"You hungry?"

Paige hesitated. Her heart still hadn't recovered from their lunch after their museum trip. Sitting across a table from Jed a second time sounded much too intimate. Especially after their little shopping experience. She hadn't had that much fun in some time.

Never could she have imagined Jed Gilbertson swapping his jeans and boots for flared polyester.

She worked to suppress a giggle.

"What's so funny?"

Taking the hand he offered, she climbed into his truck. "Just thinking what a girl could do with thrift-store-shopping photos." She held up her phone and wiggled it.

His eyes widened. "You didn't. You wouldn't." He reached for it.

She inhaled sharply, her pulse accelerating as his gaze held hers.

He stepped back. "On second thought, I should get back to the theater."

She straightened and nodded. "I should get home, too."

She would not let him break her heart again... which was the only possible way things could end.

Jennifer Slattery is a writer and speaker who's addressed women's and church groups across the nation. As the founder of Wholly Loved Ministries, she and her team help women rest in their true worth and live with maximum impact. When not writing, Jennifer loves spending time with her adult daughter and hilarious husband. Visit her online at jenniferslatterylivesoutloud.com to learn more or to book her for your next women's event.

Books by Jennifer Slattery

Love Inspired

Restoring Her Faith
Hometown Healing

Visit the Author Profile page at Harlequin.com.

Hometown Healing

Jennifer Slattery

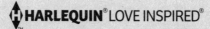

Recycling programs
for this product may
not exist in your area.

LOVE INSPIRED BOOKS

ISBN-13: 978-1-335-47942-6

Hometown Healing

Copyright © 2019 by Jennifer Slattery

This edition published by arrangement with Love Inspired Books.

® and TM are trademarks of Love Inspired Books, used under license.
Trademarks indicated with ® are registered in the United States Patent
and Trademark Office, the Canadian Intellectual Property Office and in
other countries.

www.Harlequin.com

Printed in U.S.A.

Behold, I have graven thee upon the palms of my hands; thy walls are continually before me.
—*Isaiah* 49:16

To my husband—you'll always be my hero.

Chapter One

Paige Cordell felt as if she had regressed back to that awkward, frizzy-haired bookworm who'd left Sage Creek, Texas, fourteen years ago. With no intention of ever returning.

And yet here she was. As a divorced unemployed single mother no less.

Nothing screamed failure like sitting in Mom's driveway with all of her belongings crammed into a U-Haul hitched to her car.

She glanced back at little Ava, sleeping soundly in her car seat. She looked so peaceful with her rosy cheeks, the halo of red curls and the slight part of her lips. As if she hadn't just spent nearly an hour fussing, not that Paige could blame her. They'd had quite the drive. Traffic, work zones, an accident just outside of Houston.

Her phone rang. Paige glanced at the screen. It was Mira, her old high school friend.

"Hey."

"Just checking you made it into town okay. And to see if maybe you'd like to stop by my place for a nice cold milkshake."

"Just got in." She explained the reason for her three-hour delay. "And though I appreciate the offer, I'm wiped."

"I imagine."

"And discouraged. I know I'll find another job eventually…"

"Have you prayed about it?" Mira's statement sliced through Paige like an accusation. "Might help."

"Please don't talk religion to me. Not today." She believed in God. But unlike her friend, she didn't find comfort in tossing every decision up to Him.

Besides, she and God hadn't exactly been on the best terms as of late.

"Well, like I said, this is only a hiccup." Mira's overly perky pep talk wasn't helping. "Consider this an extended vacation."

"I can't believe Ardell let me go. I mean, I get budget cuts, but why me? I was a high performer. I never missed a deadline, pitched great article ideas…"

"You'll find something even better with more job security."

Paige inhaled a fortifying breath. "You're right." She'd never allowed setbacks to discourage her before, and she had no intention of starting now. "Maybe even for a better magazine with a larger readership."

Only, *Chic Fashions* was about as big as they came. Not only was it Chicago's premier fashion publication, but it was considered the top in the nation. She'd worked long and hard to land a position with them, only to end up jobless and living with her mother.

The antithesis of adulthood.

She glanced at Mom's single-story brick house, heavily shadowed by a towering oak. Thick roots snaked through the grass, and a handful of dandelions dotted the lawn. The windows were dingy, like they hadn't been

washed in…ever, and the canary-yellow trim was beginning to peel.

Other than that, the place seemed well-kept, and the
yard had been mowed, which was surprising if her sister were right about how much Mom struggled. Hopefully Paige's arrival would help pull Mom out of this
phase she was in.

A blur of red seeped into her peripheral vision, and
she shifted to watch a shiny red pickup truck pull into
the adjacent driveway.

Her pulse spiked as a tall, broad-shouldered man
dressed in jeans, boots, and a cowboy hat stepped out
and then turned her way. "Seriously? Could this day get
any worse?" she muttered.

"Why? What happened?"

With the phone still pressed to her ear, she sank farther into her seat with no intention of leaving her vehicle.
At least, not until Jed Gilbertson was no longer standing
less than fifty feet away. Staring at her.

She turned to the box of office junk on the seat beside
her to avoid making eye contact. "Jed just pulled up at
his grandmother's." It'd been too long, and her heart had
been too shattered, for him to still have such a pull on her.

"I thought you were over him."

So did she. "That doesn't mean I want to see him."

"I doubt you can avoid that, considering the close relationship he has with his grandmother."

As did Paige. At least, she had, before moving away.
She loved that woman dearly and wanted to see her, to
reconnect—without Jed hovering nearby.

"He'll probably be paunch bellied and balding in another five years." Mira laughed. "Does that help?"

Paige envisioned him in his junior year, sneaking extra
cookies off his grandma's counter, something he'd done

often. Laughter danced in his chocolate-colored eyes, and a scruff of a beard was just beginning to fill in.

He'd filled out some since then, though he'd always been muscular, and his features had sharpened. Other than his Stetson—he'd traded his signature black one for a tan variety—he dressed as she'd always remembered. Simple T-shirt, faded jeans and boots that were scuffed and worn but not tattered.

The man who had once been her entire world. For a while, she'd thought she'd been his, as well.

She hated to admit it, but he'd only grown more attractive, while she'd noticed the first hints of crow's-feet on her own face.

"Your breakup was a long time ago, Paige. Let it go. Maybe you two can become friends again. You used to be so close. And if not, who cares? Guys like him peak in high school."

And apparently women like Paige peaked in their thirties, then regressed.

As much as she wanted to remain in her car for the rest of the evening, Paige needed to get out before she looked even more foolish than she felt. "I should probably get going."

"You've got this."

"Thanks, Mira."

"And don't forget, you, me, coffee or dinner. Soon."

"For sure."

After ending the call, she took a quick glance at her reflection in the rearview mirror. Hair the color of a new penny, in a slightly frizzed bob that cost little more. The spider veins accumulated from three nights of poor sleep contrasted sharply with her pale blue eyes. And her peach-toned skin made the flush in her cheeks all the more noticeable. She eyed her yoga pants, which were splotched with bleach stains, and cringed. Of all the times to choose comfort over appearance…

Just then, little Ava began to fuss. "Mama's coming, sweet girl." She fluffed her humidity-flattened hair and stepped out into the hot August sun. Footsteps scuffed toward her.

Ignoring the tall, handsome figure standing an arm's length away, she unfastened her daughter from her car seat and positioned the little one on her hip.

"Howdy."

She turned to find Jed looking as handsome—and country—as ever. His chocolate-brown eyes made a visual sweep of her, pausing a fraction on little Ava, before locking onto hers. "Haven't seen you in a spell. You…you look good." He lifted his hat to scratch his head, revealing those wavy chestnut locks she'd always loved. Like she'd expected, he wore his hair short, almost shaved on the sides, but longer and fuller on the top.

Heat rushed to her cheeks. "Thanks."

"Who's the little princess?"

"Ava Marie, my daughter." As if he hadn't heard all about Paige's relationship troubles and her gem of a baby-leaving ex-husband. She had to be on every prayer chain in Sage Creek, if not all of Texas.

"Need help?" Stubble covered his square jaw, and his lips curled upward in his characteristic crooked smile. The one that had captured, then shattered, her heart when she'd needed him most.

She took a deep breath, hoping her voice wouldn't reveal her rush of emotions. Emotions she'd thought were long buried. "I've got it, thanks." Then, to prove the point, she grabbed her computer bag from the back and slung it over her shoulder. "How are you?"

"Oh, you know, same ol', same ol'."

His response provided the perfect end to an awkward conversation. She forced a smile. "If you'll excuse me…"

Little Ava squirmed in her arms.

He eyed her U-Haul. "You moving back?"

She swallowed but held his gaze, though his question zeroed in on all of her insecurities.

Divorced.

Rejected.

Discarded.

Proving she stunk at relationships. And choosing men—something she'd do well to remind herself of every time Jed's deep brown eyes spiked her pulse.

"For a while. To help my mom." Which was true. He didn't need to know the rest. "How's your grandmother?"

"Putterin' around, as ornery as ever. She'll be glad to see you. Does she know you're back?"

Paige gazed toward Mrs. Tappen's house. "Probably." Her mom likely mentioned something to her. Still, Paige really needed to stop by, see how she was doing.

"Bet she'd even make a batch of those snickerdoodles you always loved."

The mention of her favorite cookies brought back a slew of memories—of her sitting at Mrs. Tappen's breakfast counter with her cold hands wrapped around a hot mug of cocoa that was topped with miniature marshmallows. Of her parents' fighting, the reason Paige had always ended up at the sweet woman's home. After her father had bailed and Mom had shut down completely, when Paige had been in desperate need of a friend, Jed's grandmother had opened wide her arms and her house.

But the memories that most squeezed her heart were of the hot summer nights she and Jed had sat on Mrs. Tappen's back porch, sipping lemonade. They'd talked about everything, from pop music to where they wanted to land as adults.

Back then she'd felt certain Jed's future would include her.

He stepped closer, and his cologne teased her nose. "What can I carry for you?"

"I'm good, but thank you." She marched up the walk to her mom's house, locking her car en route.

She'd unload the rest of her things later. On her own.

Because despite Jed's little welcoming act, she had no intention of being friends with the man.

Her heart couldn't take another rejection.

With his hands in his pockets, Jed watched Paige march into her house. She was more beautiful than ever. Her auburn hair, streaked with blond, was cut in one of those modern, windblown styles. Her teeth were straight and white. Way back then, she used to wear braces.

She looked classy, even in workout clothes. And for sure citified. She looked nothing like the quiet, shy teenager he'd once kissed.

If he had to do it over...

If her abrupt departure was any indication, the girl wanted nothing to do with him. Did she hate him that much, or had she simply moved on, determined she was too good, too...elegant and proper, for guys like him? But he only had himself to blame. He should've held on to her when he had the chance, been there for her. Should've stood by her and fought for her. Instead he'd been too wrapped up in his own drama. Too busy chasing the next party and running from the high-dollar, fancy life his parents tried to force on him.

He wasn't fool enough to think they could ever have anything between them again, but he hoped they could at least be friends. And that somewhere beneath her sad eyes, he'd catch a glimpse of the girl he'd fallen in love with. Did she still exist, or had city life squeezed that out of her?

Couldn't be easy raising a kid on her own. Was that what had brought her back? There'd been a time when he would've known that. When she told him everything.

Before stupid rumors and his reckless, party-chasing behavior had destroyed her trust and broke her heart. And the fact that she had believed the lies a bunch of high schoolers had spewed had broken his.

She should've known he hadn't cheated on her and never would have.

Surely she wasn't still nursing that grudge?

With a sigh, he turned toward his grandmother's house and sauntered up the walk.

Inside, he hung his Stetson on a peg near the door. The aroma of baked goods—peach pie and chocolate chip cookies, if he were to guess—wafted toward him, causing his stomach to growl. His grandmother's high-pitched voice emanated from the kitchen. She was singing a country song he didn't recognize.

Smiling, he shucked off his boots and proceeded past the formal sitting room, which was decorated with family pictures, and headed down the hall. In the kitchen, he found her at the sink with her back to him, and her hips and head swaying in opposite directions.

"Hey, Grandma."

She squealed and whirled around. "Oh, Jed! You scared me, boy." She wiped her hands on a towel, then deposited it on the counter.

He surveyed the slew of sweets occupying nearly every surface. "What's with all this? Trinity Faith throwing a charity bake sale I wasn't aware of?"

She nodded. "To help with the library's new book campaign." She grated orange peels over a cream pie. "So, what'd you find out about my grass?"

"You're overwatering, for one. The backyard was swampy wet, especially by the fence. You might have a mess of take-all patch."

"Take what?"

He chuckled. "That's the name of the fungus."

"Makes no difference what it's called. Question is, can you get rid of it?"

"I'll grab some fungicide next time I stop at the hardware store. I'll give it a good spray when I come back to mow on Saturday."

"I hate to put you out. I know you're busy with the theater and all."

"Nah, it's fine. I could use the exercise."

"How do things look for this weekend?"

His heart ached to see the worry in her eyes. She loved that dinner theater and all of the memories it represented. Seemed weird that they'd been talking about changing the name, but Murder, Mystery and Mayhem wouldn't fit their new branding. They were taking a risk, but they needed to do something.

Jed's grandfather had purchased the business some twenty years ago, and for a while it'd been thriving. The place had drawn folks all the way from Austin. But when Grandpa had gotten sick, the business had taken a hit. After he had died a few years ago, she'd fought hard to keep it, and had even refinanced her home to pay off the mounting debts. It hadn't been enough.

That was when Jed had stepped in and purchased half of the business, using the equity he'd built into his place.

"We've got quite a few empty seats left." He rubbed

the back of his neck. "But I've placed a couple ads. I'm sure things will pick up soon."

"What do you think the problem is?"

"Not sure." He suspected the place had developed a bad reputation, thanks to a string of cheesy productions put on by the former manager. Bad scripts could drive a dinner theater into the ground. Plus they'd cut corners on the menu, when she had lacked the funds to buy quality ingredients.

"We just need to figure out a way to turn things around," he said. According to Dad, a smart man would've followed his advice and finished his law degree. Joined the firm, like Jed had been groomed to do. But Grandma had needed him. Still did.

"You think your Western idea will help?"

"Hope so." It'd either save the place or shut it down for good. "You saw the estimates I forwarded you?"

"I did. That's some chunk of change."

The last thing he wanted to do was sink more money into that place, but what choice did they have?

She opened the oven, and the scent of chocolate wafted toward him.

"No hard feelings intended—" he sat at the breakfast bar "—but I don't feel our production's unique enough to draw folks in." The truth was that their show was cliché. A fancy inn with a butler, maid, waitstaff and guests.

"I get that."

"By turning our place into something rustic, uniquely Texas, we can separate ourselves from the pack. And hit the tourist market." If he could tap into some of the area's Texas pride, the business might just take off. Assuming he could transform the place on their tight budget.

She gave a brisk nod, keeping her mouth firm. "It's

time we make a change, because we for sure know what we're doing now isn't working."

"We'll have to shut the theater down during the remodel."

"When does Drake think he can start?"

"Hopefully within the next few days."

"Good." She angled her head and drummed her fingers on the counter. "Wild West Murder Mystery. This just might work."

"You don't know any scriptwriters, do you?"

"You can't find one online like we always have?"

"Haven't found any that fit my idea yet, at least none that are any good." And they were short on time.

"Hmm…" She tapped a finger against her chin, then smiled. "Matter of fact, bet you Marilyn's daughter could help us out. I told you she and her little one were coming for a visit, right?"

"Nope."

The twinkle in her eye said she'd withheld that tidbit intentionally. Why? Was she worried he'd try to avoid her if he knew? Or that he'd chase after her and maybe hurt her more than she already was?

His grandma had said Paige's divorce had hit her pretty hard.

He grabbed a candy from a dish on the counter. "But I figured that out quick enough when I saw her sitting in her car in her mama's driveway."

"She's here already? Oh, how wonderful." Grandma scurried to the pantry and brought out flour and sugar. "You remember she's a writer?"

He nodded. She'd always said she wanted to be a journalist someday. Had even submitted a few things to the school paper. But there was a big difference between news stories and script writing. Not to mention, she'd seemed to cart quite the grudge back into town. He wasn't so sure she'd lift a finger—or pen—to help him.

Though, she just might help Grandma…

He popped another candy into his mouth. "Doubt she'd be interested. We can't pay much. Plus we need something pretty quick."

Grandma pulled what appeared to be her last baking dish out of the cupboard. "Well, at least talk to Paige. It never hurts to ask."

"I guess." She was as apt to take the job as a heifer was to eat moldy grain.

"And bring her a nice fresh plate of cookies while you're at it. To welcome her home. Matter of fact, I'll come with you. Soon as I'm done baking these snickerdoodles. Those always were her favorite, you know."

He did. He knew almost everything about her. At least, he had, back in high school. But it'd been fourteen years. She'd probably changed a lot since then.

He had half a notion to find out just how much.

Chapter Two

Paige deposited her suitcase on the entryway floor, blinking as her eyes adjusted to the dim lighting in her mother's home. The place smelled like eucalyptus and peppermint.

"I'm so glad you're here." Mom rose to meet them and instantly took Ava from Paige's arms. She gave her a squeeze, then blew raspberries into her neck, producing a high-pitched squeal. "A child needs to be near her grandma. Why, she's almost three years old, and I could count on one hand the number of times I've seen y'all."

Paige studied her. "How are you?" She'd dyed her hair nearly black, but two inches of gray roots showed. She'd lost weight, giving her face a pale, sunken appearance, and dark circles shadowed her golden eyes. "Stacy says you're not sleeping?" Her sister had also told her the doctor indicated most of Mom's health issues were most likely psychosomatic. What did that mean exactly, and how could Paige best help her? Or, at the very least, not make things worse?

Mom waved a hand and shifted Ava to her other hip. "That's the least of my problems." Moving into the living room, she stepped over a box of papers on her way to her recliner. "The good Lord knows I've got plenty of other things to tackle, like my chest pains and breathing issues."

She grimaced and sucked in a series of quick, shallow breaths. "Been to more doctors than I can count, and not a one of 'em can figure out what's ailing me. Some days I'm so tired, it's all I can do to pull this aching body out of bed."

She sat and bounced Ava on her knee. "But enough about my health woes. Your uncle Ken called. To check on how you're feeling about leaving Chicago, I suspect."

"I'll call him later."

"He said he was heading out for a business trip but would call you next week sometime." She eyed Paige's things. "That all you brought?"

"I'll unload the rest later." When she was certain Jed wasn't around. Obviously she couldn't avoid him forever, not with his grandmother living next door. But she could delay their next encounter, at least until she had a better handle on her feelings.

After fourteen years, she was starting to wonder if that day would ever come. She'd expected to feel awkward seeing him again. But she hadn't anticipated how raw her emotions would be.

Then again, she'd been through a lot over the past year and a half, first with the divorce, and now losing her job and having to move… Her recurring bouts of insomnia certainly weren't helping.

Crossing to the green couch, she glanced about at the mess. Papers piled on a rudimentary desk shoved against the wall, a mix of clutter crowding out the old computer.

A foot or two away stood a metal folding chair that had a torn seat cushion with wads of paper scattered near its legs and overflowing a plastic garbage can. Next to this,

Mom had stacked manila folders, notebooks and what looked like medical dictionaries. Had working from home been good for her? Or had it allowed her more time to obsess? If only Paige knew how to help her.

She kicked off her shoes. "How's work going?"

"Busy. Stressful. It's not helping my health issues—that's for sure." She started talking about a slew of tests her latest doctor had given her. "If they don't figure things out soon, I may need to find me one of those specialists they got in Houston. Though I imagine they cost a pretty penny."

Paige listened, but other than with the occasional "Uh-huh" and "I'm sorry," she wasn't sure how to respond.

The doorbell rang, and she raised an eyebrow. "You expecting someone?"

Mom huffed. "Probably one of those cleaning-supplies salesmen. Last thing I need is more lemon-scented spray bottles under my sink."

"I'll get it." Paige opened the door to find Jed and his grandmother standing shoulder to shoulder on the stoop.

"Oh, sweet Paige, it's so good to see you." Mrs. Tappen swooshed inside, set the plate of cookies in her hands on the entryway console and then swept Paige into a tight hug.

The familiar scent of her almond-cherry lotion warmed Paige's heart. And almost soothed the unexpected jolt at finding Jed a few feet away, waiting to be invited in.

"What a pleasant surprise." Mom crossed the room. Ava ran over and tugged on Paige's leg.

"I hungwy."

Paige scooped her up and held her close.

"There's that sweet little girl of yours." Mrs. Tappen smiled and tickled Ava's ribs. "Not going to scare the poor thing by asking to hold her—just yet." She winked at Paige.

Mom laughed. "Oh, I'm sure she won't act bashful for long." She glanced at the cookies. "My, these look delicious. Would you like some coffee? I can make some right quick. My heart's been giving me fits, racing for no good reason, but my hands work just fine."

"I'd hate to put you out."

"Not at all." Mom led the way to the kitchen. Mrs. Tappen followed, leaving Jed and Paige in the living room, staring at one another. Ava began to squirm. Paige set her down and she scampered after her grandmother, calling out, "Me some? Pwees? Me want some."

"Hey." He hooked his thumbs through his belt loops. "Long time no see, huh?" He gave a half-hearted chuckle.

"Right." She followed his gaze to a mound of what she hoped was clean laundry, piled on one end of the couch. If he and his grandmother had called first, she could've cleaned up some.

"Have a seat." She motioned toward a plaid love seat with sunken cushions, made sure Ava was occupied with some toys and then followed Mom into the kitchen.

"Grab some napkins or something, will you, sweetie? For the cookies." Mom filled a dingy coffee carafe with water, which she then poured into the percolator. She faced Paige with her hands planted on her hips. "Have you had supper?"

"We had plenty of snacks on the drive." Paige grabbed four dessert plates from the cupboard—using just napkins felt too…shabby. Whenever she'd been to Jed's place, which had been a total of three times back in high school, all she'd seen was fancy china.

"I've only got peanut butter and corn chips in the pantry." Mom swiped hair from her face with the back of her hand. "I meant to go shopping—wanted to cook up some steak and potatoes, along with baked squash for little Ava. But I just didn't have the energy. I told you how tired I get."

Paige nodded. "I'll go tomorrow, Mom. No problem." She'd do an inventory of her mother's cupboards in the morning. Then she'd stock them up with healthy foods. Was she eating well? Getting out of the house? Spending time with friends?

"You should've told me you were running low on groceries." Mrs. Tappen frowned. "Jed would've picked up whatever you needed. Matter of fact, write him up a list. He's grabbing a few things for me tomorrow—he's sweet like that."

Mom poured four cups of coffee and then placed them on a porcelain tray, one of the few nice serving sets she owned. "You're lucky to have him so close by." She led the way to the living room.

Paige followed to the archway that signaled the end of the kitchen, and then she stopped short. Jed was sitting on the ground, next to Ava, and had begun playing with her grungy stuffed cat, talking to it as if it were real. The image triggered memories of dreams—of her and Jed and their happily-ever-after—she'd long since let die.

She could not—would not—allow them to resurface. Two heartbreaks in one lifetime were more than enough. Besides, by summer's end, she'd be back in Chicago with its museums, restaurants and shopping malls.

Upon seeing Paige, he stood and sort of hovered there, as if uncertain where to land. He eventually chose the edge of the couch where her mom hadn't piled laundry.

Paige took his place on the floor, largely to distance herself from him.

She grabbed some board books from her backpack and

handed one over. Ava started flipping through the pages, repeating random words from memory.

That entertained the adults for a bit, but soon the conversation, which had already felt stilted, stalled.

Jed shifted. He scratched at the back of his neck, looked at her and then at Mom with his brow pinching in that way it always did when he was trying to come up with something to say but had reached a blank. But then he grabbed a cookie and shoved half of it into his mouth.

Paige was tempted to do the same, if only to distract herself from the much-too-handsome man sitting in her mother's living room.

It was almost like old times.

But if her divorce had taught her anything, it was that she had no business dabbling in romance. The deeper one fell, the more it hurt when everything came undone. And based on the way her breath stalled every time his chocolate eyes latched on to hers, she was dangerously close to regressing back to her teenage years, when Jed's crooked smile and laughing eyes had threatened to steal her reason. She'd responded to her ex-husband in much the same way and had allowed his sweet talk and promises of forever blind her to some major red flags.

Mrs. Tappen folded her hands in her lap. "Not sure I'm used to seeing you all grown-up, Paige. I still remember when you were a freckle-faced youngster who could never decide if you wanted to play the dainty little princess or go prancing through the mud."

Paige offered a slight smile.

"Seems to me, she always had an instigator," Mom said.

Mrs. Tappen eyed Jed. "Oh, there's no doubt about that. 'Course, I don't remember her putting up much of a fight when it was all laid out on the table." She shook her head. "Still can't believe those two went diving in that stinky old pond, looking for buried treasure of all things."

Mom laughed. "Took three cycles in the washing machine to get that smell out those jeans of hers. I had to throw Paige's brand-new sneakers away."

Jed had thought that was the funniest thing—at least he'd had the sense to take his shoes off before diving into the muck. Back when they were best friends. Before things had turned romantic and then had ruined everything. She glanced his way to find him looking at her with an intensity that unnerved her.

Averting her gaze, she cleared her throat. "That was a long time ago. I've since given up my affinity for dirt." She wasn't up for any more treks down memory lane— of talking about the "good old days" when she had spent almost every free moment with Jed, the first man she'd ever truly, fully given her heart to.

Other than her daddy—the first man to leave her and break her heart.

Had every male relationship she'd developed ended in pain?

Mrs. Tappen smiled. "I see that. You've grown up right beautiful. And that child of yours is precious." She faced Mom, and her expression sobered. "How you been feeling, Marilyn?"

Mom sighed. "My stress level is through the roof. Not only over my health, which is enough to knock any woman down, but work's been busy, too." She rubbed her temple. "Sure wish I could be more like Paige with nothing to worry about other than what to eat for lunch. I keep telling her to enjoy herself a bit, but she insists on following that silly planner of hers. She has everything scheduled to the half hour. Isn't that right, honey?"

Her cheeks flamed. As soon as this conversation

ended, she and Mom needed to establish some boundaries regarding what could and couldn't be discussed in
front of Paige's ex-boyfriend.

"So, Paige…" Mrs. Tappen wrapped both hands
around her coffee mug. "What have you been up to?"

Mom brushed cookie crumbs from her hands. "I told
you she lost her job."

"Mom!"

"What? It's the truth. And you have absolutely nothing to be ashamed of. That boss of yours did you wrong,
honey. Her and all those suits-and-ties in that big, fancy
high-rise you worked in wouldn't know a talented writer
if she landed smack in their lap."

"Ardell didn't have a choice."

"Budget cuts." She scoffed. "Right."

"Their loss—our gain." Mrs. Tappen smiled and cast
a veiled look toward Jed.

"No truer words, my friend." Mom stretched her legs
out in front of her and crossed her ankles. "I'll for sure
enjoy having her around. But I have a feeling she won't
be putting down roots here, not unless one of us can do
some strong convincing." Her face sobered, and with a
deep breath, she fiddled with a button on her shirt. "As
much as I'd love for her and little Ava to stay, her heart's
in Chicago."

Paige watched Ava occupy herself with the buckles
on her backpack. Could this conversation get any more
uncomfortable?

"It's such a shame they couldn't find some way to keep
you." Mrs. Tappen pulled her long braid over her shoulder and tugged at the end, twisting it around her finger.
"Your mama told me all about it. If you ask me, seems
they could've at least moved you to another department."

Paige shrugged. It wasn't like they could've offered her an accounting position.

"I agree," Mom said. "Staff reduction, my big toe." She slapped her thigh.

"Mom, please." Based on the heat radiating from Paige's neck, she feared she was beginning to turn blotchy. Lovely. Now seemed like a great time to leave the room, but leaving wouldn't end this incredibly embarrassing topic of conversation. It'd only prevent her from knowing what had been said.

"It's true, and by no fault of your own, I might add." She faced Mrs. Tappen. "Girl worked hard for that magazine. Barely had time to herself. Hasn't dated in…what? Over a year."

That was the last straw. She grabbed her wallet from her backpack and stood. "I hate to dash out like this…" All eyes shifted her way. "Can you watch Ava for a bit?"

"You're leaving so soon?" Mrs. Tappen scooted to the edge of the couch cushion.

"I've got…" She'd never been a good liar, and had no intention of becoming one now. But neither did she plan to sit here, while her Mom openly discussed her failures. "To pick up a few things." Which was true enough, if she wanted to feed her daughter something other than corn chips and peanut butter for supper. Maybe she'd buy a tub of ice cream for herself while she was at it. Chocolate fudge macadamia with brownie chunks. "I'll see you later."

"Wait, please." Deep lines etched across Mrs. Tappen's furrowed brow. "I— *We've* been wanting to speak to you regarding…" She looked from Paige to Jed, then back to Paige. "I…er… What I mean to say is…" She nudged Jed. "Did you have a question, dear?"

He blinked. "Question?" He cleared his throat and

stood. "Right. I…um…" He stepped forward. "Can I call you? Maybe we could meet? For coffee? I'd like to talk with you about something."

She studied Mrs. Tappen. "Are you feeling all right?"

She laughed. "Oh, nothing like that, dear. Jed here's just got…an idea, is all."

Paige wasn't sure she liked the sound of that.

"You know where to find me." She forced a smile, but it felt wobbly. "Now, if you'll excuse me, I really do have things I need to attend to."

Chapter Three

Late Friday morning, Jed met his contractor friend, Drake Owens, at the theater, to get an estimate on the needed renovations. Seemed he wanted to make more changes than he had the money for.

"I know this isn't what you wanted to hear," Drake said as he tucked his pencil behind his ear. "And of course this is all a guestimate. Won't have real numbers till I price things out. But based on your budget, it's fair to say you're going to have to make some choices."

Jed rubbed the back of his neck. "Sounds like I need to separate the must-dos from the want-tos." The carpet was top on the gut-it-and-burn-it list. Maroon with a gold paisley pattern, darkened to a dingy yellow in high-traffic areas. The chairs and wallpaper, both a faded burnt yellow, needed to go. The stage could use new paint, maybe new flooring. Then there was the lobby. And the outside. Plus he'd need a new sign.

Was he foolish trying to turn this place Western? Everything was costing much more than he'd expected, but if he could do some of it himself… And maybe if he got a few of his buddies to help…

His thoughts drifted to Paige and the job offer

Grandma wanted him to give her. That'd add yet another expense, and probably more than Grandma had
considered. With all of Paige's big-city experience, she'd
probably want a paycheck to match it.

One they couldn't afford, no matter how many ways
Grandma crunched the numbers. Even so, he had to try—
had to ask Paige. Grandma wouldn't let up until he did.

He cracked his knuckles one at a time. "How's the
bed-and-breakfast-ranch deal coming?"

Drake gave a one-shoulder shrug. "Slow but steady.
You oughta stop by sometime and see what Neil's got
planned for that adventure/training course of his. That
guy's got one creative imagination."

"Might need to." Hopefully his friend's business ven-
ture would bring in tourists—the kind who liked murder-
mystery dinner theater. "Thanks for coming." He shook
Drake's hand.

"My pleasure. I'll be in touch."

Jed nodded and walked him out. As he was returning to his office, his chef called to him from the kitchen
doorway.

"Coming." He followed the scent of freshly brewed
coffee. "What's up?"

Decked in a stained apron and the toque he insisted
on wearing, Dillon Tedford stood with his backside resting against the edge of the worktable. "We've hit a few
snags."

"Such as?"

"The asparagus is nasty. We can't serve it."

"Great." Jed sighed. "Can you substitute summer
squash?"

"Don't have any, but I've got some canned beans in
the pantry."

"We talked about this. Fresh produce. Quality meat."

He couldn't elevate guest opinions of the place otherwise. "Guess you'll have to hit the store. And see if you can get a refund on the rotten stuff." He should've checked the produce when their supplier had dropped it off. Now it would cost double what they'd budgeted for.

Jed glanced at the meal-plan calendar on the wall. Some nights Italian, and others Mexican. Hard to establish any sort of brand when their dishes were all over the place. He needed to talk to Dillon about the menu changes he wanted to implement once the renovations were complete, but based on the man's scowl, today wasn't the day.

"I'll let you get to it, then." As he turned to leave, his phone rang. He pulled it from his back pocket. His mom. He answered en route to his office. "Hey. Sorry I haven't returned your call."

"You're busy. I know."

"How are you? You get enough donations for the charity auction you're working on?" Their conversations always went better when he focused on her. And away from his "wreck of a life plan," as she liked to call it.

"Yes, plenty. But that's not why I'm calling."

"Okay." He shucked his Stetson, placed it on the corner of his desk and then sat behind his computer. He pulled up his emails. Hopefully he'd received those Gold Rush script samples he'd requested. What he really wanted was a train heist, but he hadn't found anything like that. Would Paige be able to write what they needed in time for the reopening? If he didn't land on something by mid-week, he'd have to make do with what he could find. And soon, so his cast had time to rehearse.

"Your father cut his trip short. He'll be home this weekend, and I'd really like us to go out to dinner. As a family. It's been so long since we've all been together."

"I love the idea, but I've got a show both nights. You know that."

She let out a long sigh. "Well, I'm sure you can miss one. Rhonda said she drove by last Friday and the parking lot was nearly empty."

"We're doing fine." At least, they would be. Once he revived the place.

"Well then, there shouldn't be a problem with taking the night off."

"Actually, there would be. As part owner, I need—"

"The place won't fall apart if you step away for an evening. Your grandmother's quite capable. I'm sure she'll be able to manage things on her own."

No, she couldn't; otherwise he wouldn't have needed to help her out. But he didn't want to admit that to his mother.

"I just wish you'd go back to school and finish your degree, Jed."

"I did—in business. Which I'm utilizing now. Tell you what. Why don't you and dad come out here this Friday, on me? We'll grab coffee and dessert after."

"At the theater, you mean?" Her voice sounded pinched. Was she envisioning herself serving dinner guests while wearing a waitress's uniform? "No, no. I appreciate the sentiment, but your father will be tired, I'm sure. He'll want a much quieter environment."

"Some other time, then." He ended the call and set his phone on his desk. He knew his mom was just worried about him, though it'd be nice if she were a little more supportive regarding the dinner theater.

Had Paige stopped by his grandmother's yet? To snag a cookie or mug of hot cocoa, like old times? Grandma would be happier than a calf in the clover patch if Paige brought that giggling little one of hers. Ava. She had her mama's nose, slender but round as a button at the end. Her curly hair, too, like shiny copper coils. And a mischievous glint in her eyes that reminded him of Paige.

A smile tugged as he remembered her from high school, always thinking up something fanciful. When she wasn't hunched over a book. He'd been a fool to let her go. Maybe if things had been different for both of them, he never would have. He doubted there was any chance of them rekindling what they had, but hopefully they could rebuild the friendship.

On Saturday morning, Paige sat on the living room floor with Ava snuggled in her lap. Toys and books were spread out to her left, and her calendar and notes to her right. Still dressed in her pajamas, she checked the time and then her agenda, and penciled in her day planner. At some point, she needed to send out article queries and follow up on all of the places she'd sent her résumé.

"Mama, pway wiff me?" Ava held out a doll with blue hair.

"Sure, baby. Who am I?"

She scrunched her neck into her shoulders and put her arms out in the most adorable "I don't know" pose.

Paige laughed and kissed her cheek. She smelled like peanut butter and strawberry shampoo. "How about I be the mama and you be the little girl."

"Uh-uh. Me big giwl."

"That you are, and an adorable one at that." She gently tugged on her big toe.

The one highlight of her unemployment—more time spent with her daughter. And her mom.

She glanced toward the kitchen and the sound of clanking dishes. Though she still didn't understand the hypochondria, or whatever the doctors called it, and

hadn't a clue how to help, she was here. She had to believe that meant something.

A low rumble outside caught her attention. It sounded
close, like in Mom's yard.

"Oh, no." She glanced toward the living room windows. The blinds were lowered. "Please don't tell me…"
She sprang to her feet, crossed the room and parted the
blinds to see out. What in the world?

Jed Gilbertson was mowing Mom's yard. What was
he up to?

"Hold on, sweet girl." She kissed Ava's forehead.
"Mama will be right back."

She hurried outside, stopping a few feet from Jed and
his lawn mower. Close enough that bits of grass flew
back at her, causing her to sneeze.

With his back to her, he remained oblivious to her
presence.

Dressed in cut-off jean shorts, a gray T-shirt that
stretched across his muscular frame, a straw hat and—
boots? Who wore boots with shorts? Didn't matter… He
looked amazing in them.

She shook her head. She wasn't a stupid teenager anymore, and she would *not* go all goo-goo eyed for this man.
She'd had enough heartbreak in the past couple of years
to last the rest of her life.

She waited for him to notice her.

He did on his way back. Releasing the lever, he let the
mower die, then removed his hat and wiped his sweaty forehead with a bandana he fished out of his pocket. "Howdy."

"Hey." She shifted and brushed grass flecks from her
face. "I…um… I don't want to sound rude or anything,
but…what are you doing here?"

"Mowing your mom's yard."

"Why?"

"I do it every Saturday. On account of her being ill and all."

So he thought Mom was sick. Like sick-sick. And there was no way she could correct him without embarrassing her. Or herself. "That's very thoughtful, Jed, but I can take care of this."

"You sure?"

"Yeah." Her eyes started to itch and water, probably due to the grass dust that had bombarded them. She swiped the ends of her fingers under her bottom lashes. Oh. She wasn't wearing makeup. Feeling her face heating, she cast a glance at her pajamas—froggy boxers with a mismatched, baggy T-shirt decorated with a big old coffee stain. And her hair…

She touched her curly—and no doubt frizzy—locks and winced.

Too late to hide under a rock now. Straightening, she raised her chin and forced a confident smile. "I appreciate your thoughtfulness, but it's really not necessary. I'll manage my mother's yard work from now on." Or at least for as long as she stayed in Sage Creek.

"You got a mower?"

"What? Of course." She glanced toward the garage, which was closed and likely jam-packed with Mom's clutter.

She left Ava well occupied by her mother and returned less than ten minutes later. Dressed in jeans and a T-shirt, and with her hair tamed by curl cream, she pushed a rusted mower with cobwebs clinging to it. The thing had to be at least twenty years old, and probably hadn't been used in twice that time. She pressed the little gas button thingamabob numerous times, widened her stance, grabbed the lever and cranked.

Nothing. Not even a putter.

She tried several more times, jerking faster and faster, until her hands felt slick and sore. Same outcome. She studied the contraption. Then cast a nervous glance Jed's way, grateful to find him focused on mowing his grandmother's yard.

She turned back to the hunk of metal that was causing every last drop of her patience to evaporate. Stupid thing was probably broken. Now what?

The steady hum drifting from Jed's direction stopped, and she stiffened. She squeezed her eyes shut, then gritting her teeth, gave the lawn mower's lever another hearty yank.

Nada.

From the corner of her eye, she saw Jed approach with his cedar-citrus scent preceding him.

"Need a hand?"

She smoothed rogue strands of hair from her eyes and faced him with what she hoped to be a casual smile. "I appreciate your concern, but…" What? She had this handled? Obviously not.

His crooked grin sent a jolt through her. "As stubborn as ever, I see."

She crossed her arms. "As cocky as ever, I see."

He laughed, and his chocolate-brown eyes danced. "Let me take a look."

She stepped aside to give him access to the contraption, and then she waited while he gave the mower a thorough once-over.

After a few minutes, he straightened and dusted off his hands. "Out of gas."

Great. But at least it wasn't broken. "Thanks. Guess I better fill it, then." Did Mom even have one of those portable gas cans? She stepped toward the house to grab her keys, knowing full well he'd likely mow Mom's lawn while she was gone.

* * *

Shaking his head, Jed watched Paige pull her car out of the driveway and exit the neighborhood. That girl was as bullheaded as…as a…as a bull. But a whole lot cuter. Especially when annoyed. Not that he intended to provoke her, except maybe by tackling her mother's lawn before she returned.

Now, there was a challenge.

Then, once she'd calmed down a bit—she never had been good at accepting help—he'd mention the script-writing job. Or send her to Grandma's. No. As tempting as it was to pass the buck, he wasn't going to chicken out on this one.

Why was he so nervous to talk to her? He'd never been this way before…except during that summer when he'd first realized he'd fallen in love. Man, he had been a wreck, stumbling over his words and blurting out stupid, nonsensical statements. When he'd finally mustered up the nerve to ask her out, he'd botched it so badly, she'd laughed.

In the most adorable, shy way.

Then she said the word that practically made his heart spring from his chest—*yes*.

Moving quickly, he pushed her rusted lawn mower aside, then started up his. He'd made it three-quarters of the way through with sweat trickling into his eyes and down his back by the time she returned. But rather than quit, he stepped things up, as if daring her to stop him.

He made a sharp turn at her fence and almost laughed out loud. This was more fun than calf wrangling. He cast Paige a glance as he maneuvered around the thick, protruding roots of her mama's oak tree, feeling amused to find her standing in her driveway. Watching him. A red gas can sat at her feet. It looked brand-new.

Once finished, he lifted his hat and mopped his face with his bandana.

Fighting a victorious grin, he sauntered over to her. "I normally weed eat every other Saturday. I'll take care of that next time."

"It's really not necessary." The sun lit her peach complexion and highlighted the most endearing splatter of freckles on her nose and forehead. "And thank you."

"My pleasure." He hooked his thumbs through his belt loops. "So, how long are you staying?"

"At my mom's, you mean?"

He nodded.

Her gaze dropped. "Awhile."

Tight-lipped, just like she'd been at the house. Everything about her, from the hard glint in her eye to her stiff stance, said "back off." But he couldn't do that. Not yet.

"Listen. About your job…" Probably not the best intro. "You remember my grandparents' theater?"

She nodded, raising a hand to shield her eyes from the sun.

"We're partners now, Grandma and I, and we'd like to hire you on. As a writer. If you're interested." He told her about his renovation plans and his difficulties finding a workable script. "Can't pay you a whole lot, unfortunately…"

"I appreciate the offer, but…" She lifted her chin. "I'm a journalist. What makes you think I could write a mystery?"

"You won that short-story contest in junior high." She'd written a modern-day *Peter Pan* meets *Cinderella* love story.

"That was a long time ago."

"Thought maybe you could give it a whirl. If it doesn't work out, no harm done." Except then they'd be out of time and without a script.

"I don't think—"

He raised a hand. "You don't have to answer now. Just chew on it."

She gave a slow nod.

With his hands in his pockets, he watched her a moment longer. Long enough for three cars and a bicyclist to pass through his peripheral vision. He knew, because he counted, while trying to ignore the pull of her vanilla-cinnamon perfume and blue eyes.

"'Spect I should let you go." With a tip of his hat, he left, before things became any more awkward. It felt like high school all over again, only harder, because now a canyon of confusion and misunderstanding stretched between them.

Two hours later, he arrived at the theater a few minutes before rehearsal to go over the night's menu with the chef. They had two requests for gluten free and one for no dairy. Fresh asparagus lay on the counter, washed and ready to be cooked, and a quick glance into the walk-in verified steaks were marinating.

"Looking good." He smiled at his kitchen staff and shot Dillon a thumbs-up. Then he migrated to the dining area to wait on his cast, who should be arriving soon for the preshow rehearsal.

He made a visual sweep of the theater's interior, imagining how it would look after the renovations. Wild West Murder Mystery. The notion might seem absurd, but sometimes it took the unexpected to make things work. He smiled at Paige's old phrase, remembering the fun, giggling girl she used to be. Before life had stolen the joy from those sweet blue eyes. From what he'd heard, that ex-husband had really hurt her something awful. Lying, manipulation… Before abandoning her and her sweet little one.

What kind of father could just up and walk away from his baby girl?

Then again, wasn't that what Paige's dad had done years ago?

No wonder she acted so guarded around him.

What would it take for her to learn to trust again? he wondered.

Back in high school, when she'd first started pulling away, he'd thought she was done with him. That he'd annoyed her something fierce. He knew now she'd been hurting. And when Paige hurt, she withdrew. Pushed people away.

Kind of like she was doing now. He didn't know how to deal with her any more today than he had back then. But he desperately needed her help. So he better start learning. Fast.

Chapter Four

On Sunday morning, Paige awoke to Ava singing "Twinkle, Twinkle, Little Star." She was lying on her back on the guest bed with her arms stretched toward the ceiling, and her pudgy little hands opening and closing.

"Aren't you the cheerful little one?" Paige scooped her up and kissed her neck, triggering a series of squeals and giggles.

"You hungry?" She checked the time on her alarm clock. It was past eight o'clock—later than she normally got up. Or had intended to, thanks to a restless night spent fretting over Jed, the last person she needed to be thinking about.

"Ice cweam?" Ava's eyes held a mischievous glint, adding at least two years to her chubby-cheeked expression.

"Ice cream?" Paige asked. Ava scooted toward the edge of the bed, but Paige pulled her back by her ankle and started tickling her once again.

"Yeah!" She spoke in between her laughter.

"For breakfast?"

"Yeah. Ice cweam. Ice cweam. Ice cweam." Ava

smacked the bed with each statement, and her eyes were practically swallowed by her smile.

A knock sounded. "You up, sweetie?" The door creaked open, and Mom poked her head in.

"I am now. Isn't that right, Ava-girl?"

Her daughter bobbed her head, and her auburn curls danced against her forehead.

Paige leaned back against the headboard. "Everything okay?"

Mom stepped inside, wearing a long pink dress that hit her midshin and a shimmery cardigan. Ava's eyes lit up. She scrambled toward her grandmother's outstretched arms.

"There's my little princess." Mom peppered Ava's face with kisses, initiating more laughter.

Mom tugged Ava's pajama top, which was riding up, over her round belly. "Figured we'd go to church together this morning."

Paige rubbed her eyes. Church? She hadn't been in years, and not once with Mom. "I don't want to be rude, but… I didn't think you were into religion."

"Don't sound so enthused."

"I didn't mean it that way. I'm just…surprised."

"I go on occasion, and today seems as good as any, especially considering I actually slept some last night. Soon as my head quit feeling like it wanted to explode." She tugged on one of Ava's curls, then released it. "Figured you'd be happy with how you keep bugging to get me out of the house. Besides, thought you'd want to go. You always did as a kid."

When she'd accompanied Mrs. Tappen, Mom had always stayed home, sipping coffee and watching talk shows. Or rather, staring mindlessly at the television while some talk show host's voice dominated the otherwise silent living room.

"When's the service?"

"Nine."

That meant she had forty-five minutes to feed and dress Ava, gulp down some caffeine, tame her frizzy hair and get out the door. Not much time. Certainly not enough to send out her résumé like she'd planned.

Two cups of coffee and a shower later, she emerged from her room with damp but de-frizzed curls, and she was dressed in white capris and a flowing purple blouse. Wearing pink shorts and a matching top that was trimmed with lace, Ava looked as adorable as ever.

She was the one bright spot from Paige's failed marriage, the one good thing her ex-husband Jarred had given her.

"You ready?" Mom asked.

"Yep. I'll drive."

"Actually, we're—" Mom snapped her fingers "—hold on. I need to grab something to keep my blood sugar up." She dashed into the kitchen.

Suddenly, the doorbell rang. Who would be visiting so early on a Sunday? She found Mrs. Tappen standing on the stoop, wearing a floral dress and a pale blue bonnet. Her long silver braid was draped over her shoulder.

"Oh, good." She swept Paige into a tight hug. "I'd hoped you'd join us. And look at you!" She caressed Ava's cheek with the back of her hand. "As darling as a rosebud."

"Good morning, Judith." Mom approached them, carrying two bananas and a partially eaten bag of saltines.

"That it is." Mrs. Tappen patted Paige's cheek. She hiked her purse higher on her shoulder, turned toward the walk and cast Mom a backward glance. "You sleep well?"

"As well as can be expected." Traipsing after Mrs. Tappen, she talked about insomnia, backaches and everything else that hindered a good night's sleep.

Paige locked up and then followed the two chatty ladies with a smile. Psychosomatic or not, it was nice to see Mom so animated, so engaged. It'd be good to spend the morning with Mrs. Tappen, too.

Maybe her time in Sage Creek wouldn't be so bad, after all.

She rounded the corner to the driveway, but then stopped.

Oh, no. She should've known.

There sat Jed's truck in Mom's driveway with him behind the wheel dressed in a plaid, short-sleeved shirt. Clean-shaven, he grinned like a kid on the first day of summer vacation.

The image triggered memories of all of the times he'd pulled up in a pickup similar to this but not quite so fancy, waiting to take her to the movies or out for ice cream. Sometimes just for a long drive into the country.

He jumped out as the ladies drew near, tipping his hat first at Mom and then at his grandmother. "Howdy." He rounded his truck to open the door for them and then faced Ava. "Hey there, little princess."

Ava grinned, then turned her head away. Then turned it back, and then away again.

Jed laughed. "Peekaboo, huh?" He played along, revealing one goofy expression after another.

Ava giggled and snagged the brim of his hat, making it sit cockeyed. He plunked it on her head. Everyone laughed when it practically swallowed her. Everyone except Paige. She wasn't sure how she felt seeing the man who'd broken her heart connecting with her little girl.

Jed chuckled and put his hat back on. "Gonna have to

watch you, aren't I?" He poked her in the stomach, eliciting a giggle, and then faced Paige. "She need a car seat?"

"Oh. Right. Hold on." She paused. "Actually, how about we just follow. It'll be easier."

"Nonsense. I'll grab it." Her mom dashed to her car before Paige could argue.

Paige hadn't seen her move that fast since…ever.

This was not how she'd planned to spend her first Sunday back in Sage Creek. But she couldn't back out now, not without looking like an idiot.

So instead, she offered her widest smile, did her best to make small talk until everyone, Ava included, was settled, and slid into the passenger's seat—Mom and Mrs. Tappen conveniently occupied the back. So they could sit near the baby. Allegedly.

Frowning, she swiveled and looked at each of them in turn, noting the sparkle in their eyes.

They were up to something, and it didn't take a psychology degree to figure out what.

They could play matchmaker all they wanted. Paige and Jed were *not* getting back together. Even if she thought they held the slightest chance of starting over, which she didn't, she had a kid. What man wanted a ready-made family?

He eased into the street and then headed toward the church. "What've you been up to? Feel good to be home?"

She cast him a sideways glance, wishing she hadn't when her heart gave a lurch. "Haven't been here long. But so far everything's the same as when I left."

Stopped at a red light, he looked her way and held her gaze. "Maybe not everything."

What did that mean?

The conversation between her mom and Mrs. Tappen stilled, making Paige uneasy. Like they were all in on something and she was the odd man out. Or the target. Probably both.

Could Jed sense the tension? The not-so-subtle conniving the two older women were engaged in?

Paige watched houses blur into streaks of tan and blue outside her window. Until the uncomfortable stretch of silence became unbearable. "What about you? You working for your dad at his law firm?"

A tendon in his jaw twitched. "Nope. Got my business degree instead."

Her eyebrows shot up. "Really? What'd he say about that?"

"He wasn't too happy about it. Still isn't, but I couldn't see myself sitting in a courtroom all day, helping people fight each other. Besides, I've never been a bookworm or an orator. Seems a man needs to be both for lawyering."

"That's good. That you figured out what you wanted, I mean. Stood up for yourself." He'd always said he felt forced into a mold three sizes too small.

Mom and Ava began singing the alphabet song in the back. Jed joined in for a few lines. He shot her a goofy smile with his eyes crinkled, like he had countless times before, whenever he was on the cusp of a prank or about to share a joke. He'd always been quick to embark on some adventure, one he often tried to finagle her into.

"Are you happy?" The question came out before she could censor it, before she realized how much she longed to know his answer.

"I've been making out all right. Staying busy."

"He bought half my business." Mrs. Tappen reached forward and gave his arm a squeeze. "We're partners now, isn't that right?"

He nodded with his grin widening as his deep brown eyes swept in her direction.

"Speaking of—" his grandmother strained forward so her head poked between their seats "—didn't you want to talk with her about something?"

Jed sighed and rubbed the back of his neck. He gave another nod, slower this time. "Been meaning to—ah—to finish the conversation we started the other day."

She tensed, anticipating where the discussion was headed, as they pulled into the church parking lot. Women in pastel and floral dresses walked between the cars with their shiny-faced kiddos in tow. She recognized almost all of them.

Jed parked and swiveled to face her. "About that job... Have you given it more thought? We'd love if you'd write our scripts, press releases and other marketing stuff."

He went on to tell her about his plans to turn his grandparents' old theater, the one they'd poured their hearts into for decades, into some sort of Wild West–themed dinner theater. What did Mrs. Tappen think about all of that? If his plans failed, she'd lose her business, her husband's legacy.

"Can't pay a whole lot, but the hours would be flexible." Jed tugged at his earlobe, a nervous habit she remembered well. That was how she knew when he was about to ask her something, or to do something. Like before he'd kissed her that first time. "Imagine nothing near what you're used to. The turnaround would be pretty quick, but the work would be steady enough. We'd like to keep our shows new, fresh."

"Least it'd be something," her mother chimed in while unbuckling Ava from her car seat.

Paige winced inwardly. As true as her mom's statement was, it only reminded her of how broke and unemployed she was. But she tried to maintain a strong, confident smile.

"I appreciate the offer." She grabbed her purse from off the floorboard. "But I'm a journalist. I really doubt I have the skill set you're looking for." She reached for the door. "We ready?"

"Absolutely." Mom exited the vehicle. "Come on, pumpkin." She scooped up Ava and then lingered near Paige's door.

Jed and Mrs. Tappen got out at the same time, and the latter rounded the front of the truck.

"Just mull it over, sugar." She squeezed Paige's hand. "No need to answer today."

"I'll do that." She could think about it all day, all week for that matter. Her answer wouldn't change. If anything, the notion made her all the more determined to find another journalism job.

As much as she loved Mrs. Tappen, and as kind as her offer was, Paige refused to be anyone's rescue project.

In church, Jed tried to concentrate on the message, but his thoughts kept shifting to Paige, who was sitting between Grandma and her mom. Underneath her firm smiles and curt replies sat a deeply wounded woman, one who, if he were to guess, probably felt as if life were stacked against her.

Hadn't he said she wouldn't go for the writing gig? If not for Grandma's prodding, he never would've asked. But he'd hoped she would, if only to spend time with her. To catch a glimpse of the sweet, tenderhearted girl that chased after lightning bugs and spent hours watching for shooting stars.

He knew things had been rough after her dad had left. Her mom had slipped into a scary depression, but Paige had acted like Jed was the enemy. Or had she simply grown leery of all men, marking him guilty by association?

Didn't matter. She wasn't interested. From the sound of it, she didn't plan on sticking around Sage Creek long enough, nor could he offer her a financial incentive to stay. Not to mention she had a kid. As adorable as little Ava was, Jed wasn't ready to be a dad.

The pastor closed in prayer, and everyone stood.

"Guess that's it, then." Jed grabbed his Stetson from the pew beside him and repositioned it on his head.

"Paige Cordell!" They turned to see Lucy Carr, head of the cultural committee, heading toward them. She wore a pink dress and matching hat. "I haven't seen you in ages." She pulled a stiff-looking Paige into a hug, then grabbed hold of her hands and stepped back. "Look at you, all grown-up. I heard you and your munchkin were back in town."

Paige visibly tensed as a few of Trinity Faith's quilting gals gathered around, tossing off questions so fast, it made even Jed's head hurt.

"Where's that precious baby your mama talks about so much?"

Mrs. Cordell inched into the circle. "In the nursery. Having a blast with that mischievous grandson of yours, I imagine."

Lucy laughed. "I'll bet. Keeps his mama on her toes, that one." She faced Paige. "You and my daughter need to reconnect. Let your little ones get to know one another. Matter of fact, the Friday Faith gals are having their monthly craft night this week. You should come."

"Uh…" Paige hesitated. "What time?"

"Seven o'clock sharp. Speaking of time, I best get going. I've got a committee meeting this afternoon to talk about our plans for the annual father-daughter dance."

She hugged Paige, Paige's mom and Jed's grandma in turn. The other ladies followed suit in a comical display of Trinity Faith affection.

Jed took two steps back to avoid getting caught up in the fray. By the time all of the squeezes and goodbyes had ended, Paige looked ready to make a run for it.

Grandma must've noticed her discomfort, because she hooked her arm in Paige's. "Let's go grab that angel of yours from the nursery. Then what do you say we all go to lunch?"

"Sounds fun!" Mrs. Cordell grinned.

Paige visibly stiffened, and her gaze shot to him.

"I don't know." He had half a mind to go, just to corner Paige into relaxing some. But something told him they'd pushed her far enough already. Then again, she'd been pretty high-strung from day one. Probably on account of being unemployed and all, and with a mouth to feed. Most likely she needed time to think things through.

"We've got a show this evening." They'd added Sunday nights for the summer in an attempt to build up revenue. "I need to make sure my staff's all set up."

"Oh, posh." Grandma waved a hand. "There's plenty of time."

"If you don't mind dropping me home—" Paige smoothed a stray lock of hair behind her ear "—Ava needs a nap, and I want to send some queries out."

"Those can wait." Mrs. Cordell lightly slapped her arm. "It's Sunday. A day for rest."

"I've been resting since I got here, Mom. And contrary to what you may think, I do…" She took in a deep breath and released it slowly. "I'm sorry." She faced his grandma. "I would love to, truly, but can I take a rain check? I really should tackle my to-do list."

"Of course, dear." Grandma gave her a sideways hug.

"Next Sunday, then. That'll give you time to pencil us in your planner."

"I…uh…"

Jed bit back a chuckle to see Paige stammer, plumb out of excuses.

"And tomorrow we can talk more about the script-writing job." Grandma circled an arm around her waist and, leading a still-stunned Paige down the aisle, shot Jed a wink over her shoulder.

This time he couldn't contain his laughter. As stubborn as Paige was, she was no match for his grandmother, once she got her mind set on something.

Paige stepped into her mother's house, dropped her purse by the door and exhaled. That had been awkward, and something told her Mrs. Tappen was just getting started. Paige was tempted to avoid her from here on out, except she cared for her too much to do that. But how many ways could a person decline a job offer?

Paige smoothed a hand over Ava's soft curls. "Let's get you fed and down for a nap."

"You know," Mom said, "you should really give Jed and Judith's offer some thought."

"Mom, please. It'd never work, and I'm not that desperate." Yet.

"Maybe not, but I suspect Judith is."

Ava toddled off to her pile of toys and plopped on her bottom.

"What do you mean?" Paige left Ava to play, and then she headed into the kitchen to prepare her a snack of cheese and crackers.

Her mother followed. "You know their business is failing, right?"

"What? You can't be serious. Why?"

"Things started going south long before Jed put his money on the line. About five years ago, Mr. Tappen's kidneys went into failure."

"I remember." She'd sent numerous cards to him and his wife, and had talked to Mrs. Tappen on the phone, especially toward the end. But she hadn't gone to Mr. Tappen's funeral, and she'd always regretted that. It was the least she could've— should've—done for the sweet woman who'd meant so much to her. Who'd been there for her when everyone else, Jed included, had failed her. But she'd received word of Mr. Tappen's death while on a cruise. She had told herself there wasn't much she could do, but in truth she could've caught a plane at the next port city. But she'd been struggling with her marriage, hoping a week in the tropics would help.

It hadn't.

They'd returned, picked Ava up from Jarred's parents, and he'd walked out on her a few days later.

Truth be told, she'd always suspected he was having an affair.

"That year took all Judith's time and energy." Mom frowned. "Something had to give, so she let the business slide. By the time Ralph died, the theater was a mess. She'd landed so far in debt, she was afraid she'd lose the business and her house—that's how far tangled she'd gotten herself. She spent the next couple years trying to climb out—didn't tell anyone but me what was going on."

Paige opened an applesauce squeeze packet. "Why didn't she ask her daughter for help? The Gilbertsons have plenty of money to spare." Not only did Jed's father own his own firm, but he'd also inherited a large chunk of land that had been in his family for generations. Surely the place held a great deal of equity.

"I'm not so sure. Don't say anything to Jed or Judith,

but from what I've heard, the Gilbertsons may not be as well-off as they pretend. At least not anymore."

"But that doesn't make sense."

Mom shrugged. "Word has it Mr. Gilbertson made a series of risky and bad investments."

"You know how rumors are."

"Regardless, Judith found herself in the red, though she never mentioned this to anyone but me. She didn't want to burden anyone—you know how she is. But one afternoon, while talking to her and her grandson, I let word slip. That was all it took. He went to the bank the next day, refinanced his house and within a few short months, had become joint owner. Now that poor kid's near wearing himself out trying to turn things around."

"Are his efforts working?"

"Not sure. I mean, things are better, as far as I can tell. But I get the impression those two have a ways to go before they'll climb out of the red. I just hope they can do it before they both lose their homes. Anyway, figured you'd want to know."

"Thanks." What was she going to do now? Turning Jed down was one thing, but Mrs. Tappen needed her.

She had a lot of thinking to do.

Her phone rang. Uncle Ken. "Hello?"

"Hey, Budinsky. How's my favorite niece holding up?"

"Honest answer? I feel like I've regressed about ten years."

"Lots of folks hit setbacks. Take some time to regroup. And to enjoy your mother. She's missed you something fierce."

"I know, and you're right. Circumstances aside, it's good to be home."

"Remember that. Don't let the hard times keep you from enjoying what matters most."

When their conversation ended, she contemplated his statement. Though her reasons for being here stung, she and Ava were blessed to have this time. Not everyone had such a loving support system to fall back on.

Chapter Five

Later that evening, Mom took Ava out for a Grandma-kiddo playdate, and Paige sat in her car, parked across from Murder, Mystery and Mayhem. She felt like an army of ants had stampeded her stomach.

Why was she so nervous?

Besides the fact that she was slinking around Jed's dinner theater? But her behavior was perfectly reasonable. How could she consider working for the guy if she'd never seen his establishment or had even been to one of these dinner-theater places? Her theater experience consisted of high school musicals and a few Broadway productions in Chicago.

She gazed across the parking lot. The theater was sandwiched between Lace and Ribbons and an office-supply store in a gray strip mall. The sign had the name in bold red letters with a magnifying glass covering the top left corner of the first *M*.

Car doors slammed shut as couples got out and walked toward the entrance.

She checked her watch. Fifteen minutes until showtime.

After adding some lip gloss—not that her appearance mattered, as she had no intention of making her presence known—she took a deep breath and stepped out of her car. She marched toward the building in long strides and stopped in front of one of the tall windows flanking the door. Unfortunately, the reflection from the early-evening sun made it nearly impossible for her to see in.

She swiped her palm against the dusty glass and then pressed her nose to it with her hands on either side of her face.

"Paige!"

She spun around, face hot, to see Lucy and a handful of her quilting friends walking toward her.

"How fun to see you here." Lucy glanced about. "Where's your mama?"

"Spending time with her granddaughter."

Lucy smiled. "And eating up every moment, I imagine. You here by yourself?"

"I…uh…" She didn't want to lie, but neither did she want to get snagged into joining Lucy and her group. It'd be nearly impossible to slip in, incognito, if she accompanied the group of women. "Actually, I'm…"

"Yoo-hoo!" Luckily a woman Paige didn't recognize poked her head out of the theater door before Paige landed herself in a mess. "Pictures! Pictures! My granddaughter brought her selfie stick and wants to take pictures in front of the stage." She waved the quilting group forward.

Lucy turned back to Paige. "Want to join us?"

"Unfortunately, I can't, but thank you."

"Another time, then." She wiggled her fingers in a wave and then joined her friends.

Paige waited until they'd all gone in, gave herself a few more minutes and then followed a younger couple into a lobby area painted a burnt orange with a maroon-and-gold carpet.

A handful of women—some in dresses, and others

in slacks—perused a small gift shop to her right. Other people formed a short line to the counter, as their voices were echoing off the low ceiling.

What did the actual theater look like? She inched toward the opened double doors to the right of the cashier. Rising on tiptoe, she peered into the short, dim hallway. It ended with a sharp turn, revealing nothing.

"Can I see your ticket, please?"

She spun around to face the counter clerk, an older lady Paige didn't recognize. "I…uh…." She'd be smart to leave before making a fool of herself. But curiosity drew her—a writer's curse. "Um…can I see the buffet before I purchase a ticket?"

"The salad bar, you mean?"

"Yes, the salad bar."

The woman looked her up and down, and then motioned to the entrance.

Paige released the breath she'd been holding, feeling grateful for once that Sage Creek was a small town. "Thanks." She never would've been allowed in had this been a big-city theater.

She darted into the hallway, then slowed near the end. Palms sweaty, she peered around the corner and into a large room filled with circular tables covered in black linen. Patrons filled maybe half of the seats, sipping from plastic goblets. No way they'd be made from glass or crystal—not based on the drab carpeting and hideous wallpaper.

Holding a magnifying glass to his eye, a tall guy with a bushy gray mustache skulked around various diners. Dressed in a trench coat and tan trousers, he had to be an actor. Across the room, a woman in a red velvet gown periodically grabbed other people's drinks, sniffed them, then returned them. Another cast member. Amid all of this, waiters dressed in black made rounds, carrying pitchers of iced tea or carafes of coffee.

One of them approached her. "Can I help you find your seat, miss?"

"Actually, I was just checking out tonight's salad." She glanced around, instantly regretting her words. The salad bar stood near the far back corner, much deeper into the theater than she'd intended to go. "But thank you."

"My pleasure."

She could feel his eyes on her as she headed in that direction. Offering a forced smile to the diners she passed— in her jeans, the ones with the ripped knees, and striped canvas shoes—she hurried to the back corner. To see the lettuce.

Yep. It was green. Croutons, yep. Dressing, grated cheese, pickled beets—of course.

"Switch out the tomatoes. The ones you've got out now look past their prime."

That voice—the deep drawl. She froze, feeling her stomach diving to her toes as heat rocketed up her neck.

She spun on her heel and walked briskly to the door, using all of her self-control not to break into a run. Which she did, once she'd made it to the lobby. The ticket lady called out to her as she hurried past.

Paige quickened her step. She didn't slow down until she reached her car.

Plopping into the driver's seat, she felt her lungs strain to keep up with the oxygen demand initiated by her pounding heart.

Jed hadn't seen her, had he?

Late the next morning, Paige talked her mom into going to Sage Creek's downtown shopping area. With its independently owned bookstore/coffeehouse, family hardware, art gallery and a handful of boutiques, Paige hoped she could find temporary employment. She still hadn't decided whether or not to take the script-writing job. Did Mrs. Tappen truly need her? She wouldn't lie, but what about Mom? If it meant hooking Paige up with the man she liked to refer to as "the best catch in Texas," then maybe.

If Paige and Jed were meant to be together, they never would've broken up in the first place.

But she did need a job. And soon. Waitressing was likely her best option, though she felt bad applying for work when she didn't plan on sticking around town for long. Regardless, hardly anyone was hiring.

Paige handed Ava a filled sippy cup, then tucked her diaper bag in her stroller's basket. Hot as it was, they probably shouldn't keep her out too long.

"Why don't you apply for secretarial work?" Mom pulled a tube of lotion from her purse and squirted some in her hand. It smelled like lemon. "Typing or transcribing or something? Maybe you could even get a job with the school, answering phones or something, come fall."

"I need money faster than that. I'm trying to earn my way to a writing conference one of my coworkers told me about. It's at the end of this month, in Joliet." She left out the fact that all of Chicago's top magazines would be represented, and that she hoped to head back to the Windy City as soon as possible. Mom knew she didn't plan to stay forever, but she turned quiet whenever Paige talked about her plans to leave.

"I see." Based on her flattened tone, Mom had connected the dots on her own. "So, you want me to watch Ava?"

"Would you mind?" She'd planned to ask.

"Of course not." She sighed and brushed her bangs out of her face. "I'm not feeling so hot."

Paige turned onto First Street. "Want me to drop you

and Ava off at the bookstore so you can get an iced coffee?"

"Probably better. I don't want to overdo it and give myself a migraine."

They looped around to the bookstore. Paige walked them in and kissed Ava's cheek. "Have fun, sunshine." She stood. "See you in a bit."

"Good luck." Mom pushed the stroller after Ava, who'd already started to toddle off as if she knew instinctively where to find the kids' section. More likely she was following the scent of fresh fudge.

Paige decided to stop in Wilma's Kitchen first, and then work her way back, ending at Your Sister's Closet, a cute resale boutique.

She'd just made it to the cute little boutique when her phone rang. She glanced at the screen and answered. "Hey, Mom. You okay?"

"I lost my teeth."

"Your what?"

"Teeth. The partials my dentist gave me when I had to have two of my real ones pulled. They pop in and out like a retainer."

"Okay. I'm on my way."

She arrived to find Mom sitting in the café, talking to Mrs. Tappen.

"Paige? Over here!" Mom stood and waved her over.

"Mama!" Ava toddled toward her with one hand outstretched and a squished croissant in the other.

Paige dropped to one knee and picked her up. "You miss me, sweetie?" She gave her a squeeze and then turned to greet Mrs. Tappen. "Ma'am."

"Hello, dear." She enveloped Paige in a hug, and her almond-cherry-scented lotion elicited bittersweet memories. Then she pulled away and tucked a lock of hair behind Paige's ear. "Don't you look nice? Quite professional."

"Thank you."

"You should stop by the house for some baking sometime this week. I've got a hankering to whip up a batch of cinnamon rolls. Remember when we used to do that?"

Paige smiled. "I do. Those were great times." Those afternoons had been her lifeline. She'd arrived each time, desperate for a listening ear, and had left enveloped in love and with a bellyache from too many sweets.

"I'm praying for you." She squeezed Paige's hand.

For what? That Paige would accept her job offer, or that she'd get a job at all? "Thanks, Mrs. Tappen." She faced Mom. "You ready?"

"To leave? Oh, no. Not until I find my teeth."

Judith raised an eyebrow. "Your teeth?"

Mom repeated what she'd told Paige about her partials. "I got something jammed under them, so I took them out to swish with water. I wrapped them in a napkin and placed them right there." She pointed to the corner of the table. "When I got back from the bathroom, they were gone."

"Oh, my." Mrs. Tappen looked around—for what, Paige didn't know. Maybe she hoped to see Mom's molars lying on the floor. "Did you ask the workers if they threw them away?"

Mom nodded. "They already took the trash to the dumpster, and none of them seem keen on helping me search for them."

"Can't say that I blame them." The skin around Mrs. Tappen's eyes crinkled. "Tell you what. Jed is at the hardware store, picking something up. I'll give him a call. Boy's so tall, he could grab those teeth for you easy."

"No!" Paige blurted the word out with enough force

to turn numerous heads. "I've got it. No problem. Mom, you wait here."

She hurried out before either of them could argue and marched straight for the back dumpsters. Partially crushed boxes, bits of plastic bags and napkins cluttered the ground around them. The stench rising from them turned her stomach, but she didn't care. She practically jumped in, because there was no way she'd let Jed Gilbertson go dumpster diving for Mom's partials.

Luckily she found them near the top and returned to the café less than ten minutes later. Not so luckily Jed had already arrived and was in the middle of rolling up his sleeves.

"Look who's back." Mom grinned at her. "Did you find them?"

Mortified, Page gave a quick nod and extended her hand, revealing a wadded up napkin with shiny porcelain peeking through the gaps.

"You're such a love." Mom hugged her.

She shot a gaze to Jed to find him watching her, no doubt fighting back laughter.

"Paige." He tipped his hat. "Got what you needed?"

Could she possibly be any more embarrassed? "I did, thank you."

He reached for her hair, and she inhaled a quick breath as an old memory of his knuckles brushing her face surfaced. Then vanished as he tugged on a loose curl. She frowned and pulled back.

Mirth danced in his eyes as he showed her his fingertips, which were smudged with coffee grounds.

A shudder ran through her. Other people's trash. In her hair. No doubt she stank, as well.

"Well, isn't this nice." Mrs. Tappen grabbed Paige's

hand and gave it a squeeze. "Seems we'll get our chance to do lunch after all."

"I…uh…" She was liable to hurt Mrs. Tappen's feelings if she kept turning her down. But Paige felt much too unsettled whenever Jed was around to accept the invite. Clearly all of those nights that she'd told herself she was over him and had moved on were a lie.

"On second thought…" Mrs. Tappen rested her chin on twined fingers. "I've got some steaks thawing at home. I'd hate for them to go bad. Jed, think you could throw them on the grill for us?"

He looked at Paige with a crooked smile that caused her breath to catch. "You know I can't turn down a slab of beef."

"Well then, it's a plan." Mrs. Tappen hiked her purse higher up on her shoulder. "See you soon, sugar." With a wave, she traipsed out with Jed at her side, looking way too handsome in his boots, faded jeans and gray T-shirt that stretched tautly across his broad shoulders.

Paige waited until the two were out of earshot to ask Mom, "Why do you do that?"

"Do what, dear?"

"Share your entire life with the world."

"Judith is practically family. We talk about stuff like that all of the time. Why, she just had dentures put in herself not long ago."

"Tell your friends what you want, but please be careful what you say in front of mine."

Mom's eyes lit up. "So you and Jed have become friendly with one another again?"

"That ship sailed a long time ago." Though, truth be told, with every crooked grin he threw her way, her resolve was beginning to crumble.

Chapter Six

Jed plunked the last steak, which was dusted in Grandma's special spice mix, on the grill. Juices dripped and sizzled on the charcoal beneath, filling the air with the scent of mesquite-seasoned beef.

Thanks to a gentle breeze and overcast sky, the temperatures had dropped enough to make outdoor eating pleasant. Seemed all of the neighborhood children felt the same, based on the giggles drifting toward him.

Through the sliding glass door, he watched the ladies assemble a batch of coleslaw while Ava clanged a spoon against a pan lid a few feet away.

Paige stood at the breakfast counter, chopping a head of cabbage with her head down, intent on her task, and her auburn hair falling forward in soft waves. Every once in a while, she'd glance up, catch his eye, then quickly avert her gaze.

Like she used to do when they were studying, back when their friendship had first started to grow into something else.

The sliding glass door screeched open, halting his memory.

"Smells good." Grandma stepped onto the back porch,

carrying a bowl of fruit, which she placed on the metal table.

Ava followed not far behind her, sucking on a wooden spoon.

"Careful, little one." He picked her up before she could fall and injure herself. He placed Ava on his knee and bounced her while making clopping noises. Her laughter warmed his heart.

Grandma smiled. "Sure is nice having you both around. It's like old times."

"I'm not sure Paige would agree with you on that one."

"Give her time. She's got some things to work out. Emotions she thought she'd left behind, but slapped her smack in the face when she came home."

"Like what? Daddy issues?" The way her old man had walked out on her—that had to have cut pretty deeply. Jed never could understand how a father could leave his family like that. Abandon his daughters with little more than a casual goodbye, as if he were heading to the grocery or something.

"That, her divorce, getting laid off from work. Girl probably feels defeated and depleted."

The door behind her opened again.

Paige emerged, carrying the coleslaw, and her mama followed closely behind with a pitcher of sweet tea. He made eye contact and offered a smile. A flicker of light brightened her eyes, like he'd caught her off guard and the old Paige had peeked through. But then her guarded expression returned.

Ava clamored for her mom.

Jed handed her over and stood. "Can I help with anything?"

"You kids sit." Grandma appeared by her side. "Marilyn and I will take care of the rest. Isn't that right?"

Marilyn nodded. "I'd like to chat with you about a few things anyway."

Something told him those two were scheming about something. But that only proved how much he and Grandma needed Paige for the theater. If she was as good of a writer as he remembered—she once wrote a satirical piece that made starchy Mrs. Carmen smile—then she just might be what they needed to turn their place around.

And if she agreed to take the job? Then the real battle would start, because based on the way his pulse accelerated whenever she looked his way, he'd be fighting to keep his emotions in check. Something he for sure needed to do. If things didn't work out between them, she'd end up more hurt than she already was and Grandma would be out of a writer.

Not to mention how a breakup might affect Paige's sweet little girl. The way she always peered up at him with those big blue eyes, which were so like her mama's, suggested she'd attached herself to him right quick.

He grabbed an empty glass Marilyn had set on the table and filled it with sweet tea. He caught Paige's eye. "Glad you could come."

Ava started to squirm.

Paige set her down and then watched her scamper toward a cluster of dandelions. "I never could turn down your grandma's cooking."

"Smart woman. Bet you can't find gravy like hers in Chicago."

"That may be true, but we've got the best pizza. And gyros." She straightened her fork on her napkin. "I'm so sorry about your grandfather. How's your grandmother holding up?"

"Okay, I guess. I think maybe she's figured out a new normal."

"That has to be hard. They were together for a long time."

"High school sweethearts." Like he and Paige had been.

She must've been thinking the same thing, because she looked away and cleared her throat. "So, what's new with you? How're your parents?"

He frowned. Back to chitchat. Then again, that was probably safer. Drudging up the past wouldn't do either of them any good.

Paige eyed Ava, who was sitting on the lawn, pulling up grass by the handfuls, looking perfectly at home. Mrs. Tappen had that effect on people. Normally. But today, not for Paige.

Mom and Mrs. Tappen sure were taking their time bringing the rest of the food out. She should've insisted on helping them. In the kitchen. Away from Jed. She knew talking to him would be awkward. Painful. She had half a mind to join Ava on the grass, and yet here she sat.

Like a desperate teenager in need of attention. Hoping…for what, exactly? That Jed would show an interest in her again? Apologize for cheating on her and convince her they should try again?

It'd been fourteen years. Why the intense reaction, the ache whenever he looked her way?

Because he'd been a great friend once. Could they start over, keep things platonic? Anything more would only lead to another heartbreak, and she'd had enough of that to last a lifetime.

The screen door opened again, and Mrs. Tappen emerged, carrying a plate of homemade cookies. "I'd say no dessert till after supper—" she sct the treats in front of Paige "—but I know you've been hankering for these since you left Texas."

Paige smiled. "That I have."

Mom joined them, carrying a large bowl filled with green salad. "I'm waiting for another batch of your freshly baked parmesan-basil bread."

"Guess we'll have to do this again, then." Mrs. Tappen nudged Jed with her elbow. "Let's say grace." She extended her hands, taking Paige's in her own, and they bowed their heads while Ava chattered and chirped beside them. "Father, thank You for good friends. No, strike that. Family. Don't take biological blood to bond folks, not when we've got Your Son. Soothe whatever feelings we may have and help us to hold tight to what we got. 'Cause not everyone's so lucky. Amen."

Tears pricked Paige's eyes.

Mrs. Tappen passed her a container of steak sauce. "So, tell us about life in Chicago. What was it like writing for that fancy fashion magazine?"

"It was fun." And stressful, especially once the higher-ups started talking numbers and budget cuts, but Paige's love for writing made it all worth it.

"She did real well." Mom set her fork down. "Got free clothes, had an expense account."

"Really?" Mrs. Tappen reached for her glass. "Good for you."

Ava dropped her sippy cup and started to whine.

Jed grabbed it, handed it over and bopped her on the nose. "I always said you had a way with words." His gaze held Paige's.

His encouragement had meant the world to her. Gave her the courage to even consider a career in writing. She was grateful for that, or at least she had been. Sitting here, jobless, with a slew of rejected queries clogging her inbox, she wondered if he'd only been telling her what he thought she had wanted to hear.

What if she didn't have what it took to make it financially as a writer?

"Their loss." Mom patted her hand. "I'm sure going to miss you when you head back north. Hopefully I'll be feeling better by then, so you and your sister won't worry about me so much."

"Oh?" Mrs. Tappen straightened. "You're leaving us already?"

"I need to find employment first." She chuckled, then covered with a cough. The last thing she wanted to do was bring the conversation back to the job offer. Luckily Ava had grown restless, allowing Paige to occupy herself with motherly duties. She fished through her diaper bag and pulled out some scrap paper and chunky crayons.

"Ever consider putting down roots in Sage Creek?" Jed's deep brown eyes intensified, as if asking her to stay.

For a moment she was tempted to give in. But then common sense took over. "I love Chicago. The museums, food, the shopping."

"All that's good, but what about nature?" Mrs. Tappen pulled a sprig of grapes from the bowl. "So much concrete… Isn't right. Kids need fields to run in and trees to climb. All this fresh, clean air would do you both a world of good. I know how much you always loved the outdoors."

Paige gazed at the grove of trees encasing Mrs. Tappen's backyard. A memory of spending a lazy afternoon in the corner hammock, rocking in the shade with a book, came to mind. Her eyes had grown heavy. They'd started to droop when Jed had snuck up on her and pushed her out. She'd tumbled into the soft grass to find him standing over her with his eyes twinkling, as if he'd pulled the best prank ever.

"Remember when we tricked Andrew into cow tipping?" He gave a crooked smile.

Her laugh escaped. "He was so gullible."

"Oh?" Mrs. Tappen crossed her arms, but the curve of her lips was belying any attempts to look stern. "I don't think I heard about this one."

Mom frowned. "Please tell me he didn't go through with it. Those poor cows!"

Jed's eyes danced with mirth. "You know that's an urban myth, right? No one can tip a cow, unless maybe they bring some fellas with them."

With her napkin, Mom wiped a glob of dressing from her chin. "Why's that?"

"First off, they don't sleep standing up. Not to mention they're skittish things. Someone comes at them, and they run in the other direction—even faster when a kid starts running."

"Then hollering." Paige shook her head as images from that night replayed in her mind like a movie reel. "You'd think Andrew would've figured that out. That he would've given up chase and called it a night."

"Too stubborn," Jed said. "And a might hungry. I wagered a pizza, remember?"

She did, along with everything that had followed. "Andrew never did catch his cow."

"Nope, though not for lack of trying. Think he chased down every one he saw, darting all over the place."

"Till he tripped and fell facedown in…gunk."

Mom wrinkled her nose. "I'm sure he was none too pleased about that."

Jed chuckled. "Not exactly. He stomped off, leaving

Paige and I falling over laughing." His expression sobered, and his gaze fixed on hers.

As if he were remembering—the full moon. Just the two of them, standing under the stars.

Him turning serious as he had tugged on his earlobe and stepped closer.

Their first kiss, and the beginning of the end.

She shook the memory aside. That was a long time ago. So much had changed since then. *They* had changed.

Their lives had taken completely different turns. He belonged here, hanging out with his cowboy friends and attending church picnics. She belonged in Chicago, or New York or maybe even Denver, pursuing a thriving writing career.

First step: finding a way to get to that writers' conference.

Seemed taking the screen-writing job was her best option. Plus it'd help Mrs. Tappen out. They might even let Paige work from home. Then she could spend more time with Ava and keep an eye on her mom, as well as keep an eye out for job leads.

"Tell me more about this renovation project the two of you hatched up." Mom motioned between Jed and his grandmother with her fork, which had a piece of lettuce dangling from the tongs. "I'm trying to picture it."

"Think *Bonanza*." Jed pushed his sweet tea forward a bit. "Or like what you see in those old Western movies and TV shows. Wood sidewalks, wood everywhere, actually. Rustic furniture made from branches. Chandeliers made from mason jars."

"Won't be cheap, though." Mrs. Tappen ran her nail along the edge of the table.

Ava slid down from the table, and Paige started to stand.

"I've got her." Jed followed her to her diaper bag and

sat beside her as she started pulling one item out after another. He stacked them up like blocks. She soon joined in until they had a lopsided tower of diapers, baby wipes and board books.

"Right now furniture seems to be our biggest expense." He handed Ava a plastic cell phone, and she pretended to dial. "We can do most everything else real cheap, but chairs and tables…" He let out a low whistle. "I'd say forget 'em, but the place would look odd with what we've got now."

"We'll figure something out." The lines stretched across Mrs. Tappen's forehead, and her voice faltered softly.

Jed placed a hand on her shoulder. "'Course we will." His eyes radiated love.

Paige hated seeing Mrs. Tappen look so worried. The poor woman had already lost her husband. She couldn't lose the business they'd built together, too. Not if Paige could help it.

She folded her napkin in half, and then folded it in half again. "Do you remember Noah Williams? He graduated a few years ahead of us? Well, he would've, if he hadn't dropped out."

Jed opened a board book and stood it on its end. "Vaguely. Wasn't he that kid that always kept to himself?"

She nodded. "He runs a homeless ministry now. Teaches them to build furniture by using wood from trees native to Texas. His stuff's pretty reasonable."

Mrs. Tappen slapped a hand on the table. "Now, lookie there! Isn't God good? We've been fretting about something He already had a solution for, like always."

Jed looked at Paige for a long moment. Long enough to accelerate her pulse. "Think he'd let me pop by, take a look at what he's got?"

"I don't see why not."

"How about I watch Ava and you two go together?" Mom nudged Paige. "That way you can put a good word in."

"I don't know—"

"That's a great idea!" Mrs. Tappen clapped her hands. "Girl, I could just hug you! Now all we need is a talented scriptwriter, and we're set. Tell us if you know of one, you hear?" She winked.

Paige had a feeling Mrs. Tappen wouldn't let up until she conceded. Then again, considering all that the woman had done for her over the years, helping her out seemed the least Paige could do.

But what about Jed? Could she maintain a working relationship with him when memories from the past made her long for more?

Chapter Seven

The next afternoon, Paige bided her time entertaining Ava and tidying Mom's house while she waited for Mrs. Tappen to return from Bible study. Then, afterward, for Jed's truck to leave her driveway.

"What're you looking for?" Mom, newly awakened from her nap, stretched in the recliner.

Paige moved away from the living room window. "Nothing. Just…" She sighed and plopped onto the floor beside Ava to help her fit shapes through the sorting box Mrs. Tappen had given her. One of a handful of gifts dropped by since Paige had arrived.

The doorbell rang. Paige looked at her mom. "Expecting someone?"

Mom grinned and grabbed her purse from the floor beside her. "Probably the Carter twins selling cookies or popcorn or something."

"You don't have money for a bunch of overpriced junk food."

"When it helps the neighbor girls with their fundraising, I certainly do."

Paige sighed and shook her head. She understood—and appreciated—her mother's tender heart, but couldn't ignore the growing stack of bills on the kitchen counter. Especially considering Paige no longer had the means to help.

She opened the door to find a handful of Trinity Faith women she vaguely remembered from her youth group days standing on the stoop. The tallest of the four held a basket shaped like a bassinet and filled with random toddler items.

Paige looked from one beaming face to the next. "Hello."

"Paige!" A lady with short gray hair and thick purple glasses rushed forward and enveloped her in a hug. "So good to have you back in Sage Creek! How've you been? It feels I haven't seen you in ages."

So long, in fact, Paige couldn't remember exactly how she knew the lady—other than from church.

"Why, I remember the first day you walked into my Sunday-school class, wide-eyed, wearing your hair pulled in those cute French braids you always used to wear it in."

Mrs. Fowler? Her fourth-grade Sunday-school teacher?

The woman's gaze shifted past Paige's shoulder. Crease lines on Mrs. Fowler's forehead replaced the crinkles around her eyes. "Marilyn, how are you?"

"Hanging in there." Paige moved aside as her mom ushered everyone in.

Ava shuffled forward and tugged on Paige's leg. She picked her up and situated her on her hip. The child was still in pajamas, which were decorated with juice stains and remnants from her breakfast, but at least her face and hands were jelly free.

"Like I said before, let us know how we can help." Mrs. Fowler sat on the far end of the couch. "With meals, housecleaning…" Her gaze swept the cluttered room, and Paige's face heated.

"We appreciate your thoughtfulness and concern." She tossed Ava's tattered blanket into her diaper bag. "But I've got everything managed for now."

"Oh, I'm sure you do, dear." The lady with the bassinet squeezed Paige's free hand. "But we want to help, don't we, ladies?

"Absolutely." Mrs. Fowler nodded so emphatically, her short bangs bounced against her forehead. "We always got to look out for own."

"I love that about you ladies." Mom sat in her recliner and tucked an afghan around her legs. "What's in the basket?"

"This is for Paige." Mrs. Fowler's friend handed it over with a grin. "Some diapers…" She eyed Ava. "Though it looks like she's a might too grown for that, aren't you, little one? Lotion, shampoo, what have you, and cocoa and a magazine for her mama. Oh, and a gift card. We know how expensive kiddos can be."

"You shouldn't have." She'd never enjoyed receiving charity, no matter how well-intentioned. It made her feel incapable. Less than. She'd felt that enough growing up, when her dad had left her mom with a mortgage and enough debt to swallow her every dime for decades to come. The church had overwhelmed them with gifts, baked goods and other food items, which had carried them through a really tough time.

But it'd also led to snarky comments from her classmates, once the popular girls got wind of it all.

As an adult, Paige had vowed never to put herself in a position of dependency again. Yet here she was.

"We do this for all Sage Creek mamas." Mrs. Fowler rummaged through her purse, and then pulled out and applied what looked to be lip balm. "We're just a bit late with your welcome-to-the-world basket, is all."

"Through no fault of your own." Mom took a slow sip of tea. "Your kind gesture is much appreciated, isn't it, Paige?"

"Absolutely." She wasn't sure whether to feel touched or embarrassed. Nor did she quite know how to respond. But thankfully her social awkwardness was soon swallowed up in small talk about everything from how the Owens' ranch was getting along—apparently they were transforming the place into a bed-and-breakfast—to plans for the next community bake sale.

By the time they left, Paige had begun to remember some of the things she loved about living in a small town. Not enough to entice her to stay, mind you. But she was grateful Mom had developed such caring relationships.

She cradled a very sleepy Ava in her arms. "Seems someone's past due for her nap. I'll be back." She headed toward the bedroom.

"Let me do that." Mom hurried after her. "Grandma could use some Ava snuggles."

Spending time with her granddaughter certainly did seem to cheer her. "If you're sure…" Paige handed Ava over.

Mom nodded. "Absolutely. I've got to snatch every moment with this sweet girl while I can." And with a contented smile that Paige was beginning to see more and more often, Mom disappeared into the guest bedroom with Ava.

The door clicked shut, and Paige glanced out the window once again. Jed was still gone. She tamped down the unexpected burst of disappointment and reminded herself of all of the reasons she couldn't and wouldn't become emotionally entangled with that man. And as long as she kept their encounters brief, she could manage to avoid that very thing.

In the meantime, she planned to pop over and spend some time with that sweet grandmother of his.

She grabbed her purse and hurried across the narrow stretch of grass separating Mom's house from Mrs. Tappen's.

Standing on a sunflower welcome mat, Paige rang the doorbell.

Mrs. Tappen answered, wearing a yellow dress patterned with flowers, and her long gray hair was tied in its usual braid. "Paige, dear, come in!" Her eyes lit up, and she wrapped Paige in a tight hug. "Let me guess, your sweet tooth brought you over."

Paige laughed. "Something like that."

"It just so happens I got me a mound of dough rising in the kitchen. Was just about to take my roller to it." She led the way past the formal dining room with its pink curtains, floral wingback chairs and old family portraits, to her kitchen. "Where's that little one of yours?" Roasting beef and garlic filled the air, and old-time country music played on a small radio standing on the tile counter.

"Napping with her grandmother."

"How precious." She held a hand to her chest, then straightened and glanced about. "Soon as you wash up, I'll put you to work." She motioned to the sink.

Paige smiled. "Yes, ma'am."

"Want some cocoa?" She placed a cast-iron pot on the stove. "I could whip some up right quick with marshmallows, just like you like it."

"I'd hate to be a bother." She lathered her hands, breathing in the lilac scented soap.

"Pshaw. I'd be happy to do it." Mrs. Tappen turned on the heat and then went to the fridge. Her movements seemed slower than Paige remembered; her back was more hunched. A reminder that she might not be around for much longer.

Though her reasons for returning to Sage Creek still stung, she was beginning to count her blessings. Like spending time with Mrs. Tappen while the woman still had life to live.

Paige swallowed past a lump in her throat and dried her hands on a crocheted hand towel beside the sink. "So, what can I do?"

"Rolling pin's in that drawer." Mrs. Tappen pointed. "Table's clean. Make sure to cover it with plenty of flour. Don't neither of us want to be scraping goo off it all evening." She propped a hand on her hip. "You and your mama coming for supper tonight? Got plenty of pot roast and red potatoes to spare."

"I'm not sure." She carried the bag of flour to the table and sprinkled a generous amount on the surface. "Mom's not feeling so hot."

Mrs. Tappen faced her and crossed her arms. "That's not the why-not, and you know it."

Paige looked away. She grabbed the sweet dough and began to press it flat.

Footsteps shuffled closer, and a gentle hand landed on her arm. "Have you thought about why you're here? Not just in my kitchen, but back in Sage Creek. At your mama's."

Because she lost her job and couldn't afford to support herself? In truth, she knew that wasn't the answer Mrs. Tappen was poking at.

"Look at me, child." She turned Paige toward her and searched her eyes. "What if you're here to heal once and for all? To break free from all that pain and bitterness you keep locked inside."

A tear trickled down her cheek, and Mrs. Tappen

thumbed it away. "If you want to move forward, you're going to have to let go of the past."

Paige sniffed as more tears fell.

The front door clicked open, and she stiffened, swiping at her damp cheeks with floury hands. Probably smearing mascara everywhere.

"Near searched the entire store—couldn't find any fresh basil." Jed's footfalls drew closer. "Got everything else…" His voice trailed. Then stalled. "Paige."

She cast a quick glance over her shoulder, enough to acknowledge him without allowing him time to notice that she'd been crying. "Hey."

"You staying for supper?"

"I invited her." Mrs. Tappen wrapped an arm around her waist. "She wants to check with her mama first."

"Makes sense."

She could feel him watching her, and then he was at her side, sitting at the breakfast bar. His citrus cologne invaded her senses, and his patient presence tugged at the walls she'd so carefully erected around her heart.

Being around Jed was harder than she'd anticipated.

The last time she'd followed her heart and allowed a man in, she'd ended up emotionally and financially broken.

Her ex-husband had left her in near the exact state her dad had left her mom.

And after all of the times back in high school, while listening to her mom cry herself to sleep, Paige had vowed her life and marriage would be different.

Seemed she'd broken a lot of promises to herself.

Chapter Eight

Jed cringed inwardly as the young man on the stage fumbled through his lines. It wasn't just that he mumbled, or that he seemed to have an aversion to maintaining eye contact. Wasn't even his strange attire, though his trench-coat-over-skinny-jeans look didn't help any. What got him instantly crossed off Jed's callback list was the high-pitched snort he made every time he messed up. Every. Single. Time.

He and Shannon, the friend helping him screen potential talent, exchanged glances. Her quivering mouth indicated she struggled to maintain a straight face. That made it all the harder for him to do the same.

He coughed a few times to cover a laugh. "Thanks for coming in."

"Can I try it one more time?"

"Sorry, but we've got a lot of folks waiting in the lobby." True enough. "We wish you luck with your acting career." One of his cast members was leaving at the end of her contract terms, which was soon, and he needed to find a replacement.

Hopefully the next applicant—he glanced at her

sheet—Amber, would do better. At least she had some experience, though mostly from high school productions.

"Um, Jed?"

He looked up. Paige stood a few feet away; her posture was rigid, and her chin jutted forward, as if she were bracing for a fight. The vulnerability peeking beneath her hard exterior drew him. She clutched a leather portfolio under her arm.

"Hey." He stood and tipped his hat with a nod.

Had she come to audition? Did this mean she didn't want the script-writing gig? How'd she hear about the casting call?

He'd never thought of her as an actress. Matter of fact, he couldn't picture her standing on a stage, in front of anyone, let alone a room full of watching eyes.

He crossed the room to meet her. "Did you…uh…fill out an information sheet?"

She frowned. "An application, you mean?"

"You could call it that. It gives us an overview, lets us know your experience, availability, that sort of thing. We can't make a decision till we see you in action." He hated sounding so formal, especially when he'd been so quick to offer her a job. But this was different. He needed to know she could act before they talked terms.

"You mean read some of my writing samples?" She opened her leather binder and pulled out a few sheets of paper. "I haven't created much fiction since high school, but I wrote a short story, a romance, over the weekend." Her gaze dropped, and the most endearing pink blossomed on her cheeks. "I hope that's okay."

He studied the typed pages with a furrowed brow. "So…you're not here for the auditions?"

Her eyes widened, and the color in her face deepened.

"What? No! I'm here about the script-writing job. That is, if you still want me."

He did, and that worried him. How much of his job offer had been based on emotion? On feelings he had no business entertaining? Then again, it was Grandma's idea, not his. "I…uh…" As much as he wanted to see her involved, he needed to watch how he phrased things until he had a chance to check out her writing. He turned to Shannon. "I hate to keep our potential talent waiting."

"I can handle the auditions for a bit."

"I'd appreciate that." He shifted toward Paige. "How 'bout we head back to my office to talk."

She studied him for a moment before giving a quick nod, and then she followed him down a side hall to the tiny dark room that housed his desk and files. Entering, he flicked on a light, set his hat on the rack and opened a metal folding chair that was propped against the wall.

"Have a seat."

She did. He rounded his desk to do the same and set her document in front of him. He sensed her eyes on him as he read.

Her first sample, a short story, was a romantic comedy about a girl who introduced herself to the wrong man while on a blind date, only to discover the truth during supper. The next few pieces looked like they'd been pulled from various magazines. One explained numerous uses for coconut oil, and the other what to wear with which heel height. A third piece discussed different ways to shape one's nails.

He regarded her with a raised brow. Paige Cordell, the girl who once wanted to start a worm farm to sell to local fishermen, interested in glitz and glam? Then again, she had worked as a fashion writer. Apparently she'd changed more than he'd realized. As had he, hopefully for the better. More than anything, he wanted her to know that. To open herself up enough to get to know him again.

Maybe even…

He gave himself a firm mental shake. A work relationship and a rebuilt friendship—those he could handle. Trying for anything more would only complicate things.

He studied her as she sat tall and stiff with her hands folded in her lap. But her large pupils surrounded by her wide blue irises and rapid blinking contradicted her confident demeanor.

The woman was so beautiful. And smart, talented, determined…

That ex-husband of hers had been a fool to let her go.

He tidied her papers into a neat stack. "You're very gifted. Always have been."

"Thanks."

"So, here's what I'm looking for." He explained his theme to her. "Everything needs to be scripted, including my introduction, jokes and all. I'd like help with blogging, too. You comfortable with that?"

She nodded. "I've done humor. My blog alternates between satirical and straight-up comedy."

"True."

She angled her head. "You've read it?"

"I…uh… A little." Heat climbed his neck. "What's your price point?"

"Depends on how you want to do it—pay for the manuscript or have me on staff. You'd mentioned something about me helping with other stuff, like press releases or whatever."

Did that mean she planned to stick around? "How about we start with the script and go from there? We can work together some." The idea appealed to him more than it should have. "I'll share my vision, let you know what's feasible as far as set requests—that sort of thing. Then I'll read your first draft—I'd need it pretty quick. Like, in ten days. Sooner, if you can swing it." That way his cast could prepare for the grand reopening.

"How many words are we talking?"

"Scripts usually run about fifty pages, depending on choreography."

"I can do that."

"I'll probably want revisions."

"Of course."

"Plus I'd like your help for unexpected, midproduction changes, like if one of our cast members gets sick and I can't find a backup, or audience response isn't what we'd hoped."

"I'll need an advance."

"A what?"

"Payment up front."

"Oh." But what happened if he paid her and she didn't deliver? Or got mad and stormed out halfway through the draft?

She'd never do that to his grandmother. Even so, this wasn't something he could jump into blindly. He'd need some help figuring out the legalities of it all.

"Send me an email, letting me know how much you'd like to get paid." He handed her a business card, which she tucked into the flap of her portfolio. "I'll review your request and write up a formal contract, see if we can come to an agreement."

"Sounds reasonable."

He walked her out, feeling much too excited about the prospect of working with her. A man couldn't allow emotions to get tangled up in business matters. But so long as he kept things professional, he was sure that everything would work out fine.

* * *

Early the next afternoon, Paige sat in a booth at Wilma's Kitchen, a small diner with a working jukebox, red booths and checked linoleum floors. About the only modern thing about the place were the flat-screen televisions mounted in opposite corners. That and the playing cards tacked to the ceiling.

Two women Paige had gone to school with entered—one with a toddler, and the other a baby carrier. Upon seeing Paige, their faces lit up, and they hurried to her table. Paige stood to greet them.

"It was so good to see you Sunday!" Rissa, the taller of the two, gave Paige a hug. "I meant to get your phone number so we could do coffee or a playdate."

Paige pulled a pen from her purse, wrote down her contact info and handed it over. "How old's your little guy?"

"Two and a half."

"Not far behind my Ava."

"So it is possible to survive the terrible twos, then?" Holding her son by the wrist, she gave the squirming tyke a look of mock exaggeration.

Paige laughed. "So long as you have plenty of reinforcements."

"I do have that." Rissa hip bumped her friend, a girl two years Paige's junior. "The three of us should totally get together."

Paige smiled. "I'd like that. Mind if I invite my friend Mira to come along?"

"Of course not." Rissa's friend shifted her baby carrier to her other hand. "The more the merrier. You want to join us for lunch?"

"I'm waiting for someone, but thanks."

"Oh, yeah?" Rissa glanced toward the door. "Who?"

Heat climbed Paige's neck. "Jed Gilbertson."

Rissa's eyebrows shot up, and a slight smile emerged. "I see."

Ah, small-town life. She could just imagine how quickly rumors would circulate. "To talk about theater scripts."

Rissa gave a slow nod that indicated she was less than convinced, though Paige rambled on about random particulars to prove her claims. Soon the conversation shifted to nap times, cartoons and motherhood in general.

After a few minutes more of small talk, the ladies excused themselves to a vacant table near the back.

Paige was left to nervously sip an iced tea while she waited for Jed to show up for their scheduled meeting. What was she thinking? How in the world could she work with the man when a simple glance fired up her pulse? But she needed the money, and Mrs. Tappen needed her. At least, that was what Mom kept telling her.

Based on Jed's rapid response to the email she sent the night before, Mom's words appeared to be true enough. Paige had messaged him with a payment figure almost as soon as she'd gotten home. It'd taken Jed less than twenty-four hours to set up a lunch meeting to discuss her potential contract.

He had indicated a fast turnaround time, which could work in her favor, should he try to squeeze her.

But he wouldn't. He wasn't a user. Never had been.

With her legs crossed, she jiggled her foot, and her eyes were trained on the window, to the street beyond. She couldn't seriously be nervous. Not to meet Jed Gilbertson.

She was about to make a dash for the restroom when her phone rang. Mira. "Hey, thanks for calling me back."

"What's up? You sounded sort of panicked in your message."

"I'm about to meet with Jed." She filled her in on the details.

"Oh. The two of you reconnected, then? How'd that go?"

"Smashing. Unemployed girl begs her ex-boyfriend for a job and lands herself a heartache waiting to happen."

"You still love him, don't you?" A child whined in the background.

"No. Yes. Maybe." She sighed. "I don't know. I shouldn't. But I really need the money."

"So, now what?"

"Woman up? Act like the functioning adult I am? Then douse my highly unstable emotions in a tub of chocolate frosting."

"You'll invite me to join you for that last one, right?"

"Only if you bring your own tub."

"Which begs the question—when were you going to ask me to lunch?" The whining on Mira's end had turned into a wail. "Listen, I hate to do this, but I gotta go. The troops are getting restless."

"I understand." She ended the call in time to see Jed heading her way. Carrying a manila folder, he wore a navy shirt and faded blue jeans, and was clean-shaven.

Had he shaved for her?

Of course not. The man did pick up a razor every once in a while.

His easy smile made her heart jump. "Howdy." He removed his hat and raked a hand through his dark hair.

She cleared her throat. "Hi." She took a sip of her tea while Sally Jo, the waitress, relayed the daily specials.

When she left, Jed opened his folder, pulled out a document and slid it toward her.

The contract. "Thanks." She glanced over the first page. "You drafted this up in a hurry."

"Asked a family friend who's a lawyer to write it up. I think it's fair for both of us."

"Your dad didn't help you?"

"Nope."

Apparently things were still tense between them. Did they talk at all, or had he and his dad become near strangers? It wasn't her business. Besides, her empathy for Jed wouldn't help her maintain a safe emotional distance.

She returned her attention to the document and studied the amount offered for the script. The terms said he'd pay half up front, and the rest once she delivered the first draft, as well as royalties based on sales thereafter.

She turned the page. "For marketing pieces, I get paid by the word?"

He nodded.

The wage was less than she'd anticipated. Because he and Mrs. Tappen didn't have more to give, or because he wasn't aware of the going rate for writers? Then again, she only knew how much freelancers in Chicago got paid.

He scratched the back of his neck. "We'd love to offer you more, but we just don't have it."

"I see."

Sally Jo reappeared, chatted a bit, took their orders and then left.

An awkward silence followed.

Obviously Jed was taking on the bigger risk here. Besides, she wouldn't just be working for him. Every dime she earned would be coming from Mrs. Tappen's account, too.

She considered that and the contract terms while they waited for their food. She didn't want to appear overly anxious. It wasn't as though she had anything better to do, except gather more article rejections. Plus she truly wanted to help his grandmother out. As much as the thought of working with Jed knotted Paige's stomach—and sparked confusing emotions—it was the right thing to do.

She rummaged through her purse for a pen. "Seems fair enough." Not as much as she'd hoped, but enough to secure her spot at the writers' conference. She initialed where indicated and then signed.

"Your turn." She pushed the document toward him.

His boyish grin halted her breath. "Looking forward to working with you." His dark, penetrating eyes searched hers, as if he wanted to say more.

"Yes, well…" She fumbled for her drink.

She needed to find a way to get hired on somewhere permanent. In a city with nice restaurants, lots to do, and with lots of potential stories, fashion or otherwise, to write on. Because the longer she stayed in Sage Creek, the greater the threat of heartbreak.

Chapter Nine

Jed would arrive at any moment.

Paige fought the urge to pace, or check her appearance in the mirror for the tenth time. She found her nervousness infuriating. After fourteen years, one would think she'd long since moved on. But when his dark brown eyes latched on to hers, and he offered her his crooked, boyish smile, her insides turned to jelly. Which was why she should've insisted on meeting him at the furniture place. If she had thought New Life Furnishings would show up on Jed's GPS, she might have.

She'd soon spend nearly two hours alone with the man. What would she say?

What if his emotions were as jumbled as hers, his memories as sweet, and he initiated one of those conversations?

Did she want him to?

What she wanted was to return to Chicago. She could never support herself and Ava in Sage Creek—at least, not doing what she loved.

An engine hummed in the driveway. She gave Ava a squeeze and grabbed her purse. "Be good for Grandma." She looked at her mom. "I shouldn't be long."

"I'll probably spend most of the day in bed anyway." She rubbed her temples. "See if I can't sleep off some of the ache in my bones."

Paige bit her bottom lip. "What about Ava? You sure you're okay watching her?"

"Some grandbaby snuggles will do me good. Besides, it doesn't take much energy to read stories." Mom waved a hand. "Don't worry, nap time will come soon enough."

The doorbell rang. Expelling a sigh that did nothing to calm her jittery stomach, she answered the door. Jed stood on the stoop, looking way too good in snug jeans, a T-shirt and his Stetson.

"Hey." She offered what she hoped to be a confident, nonchalant smile.

"Howdy. You ready?"

She nodded, slung her purse over her shoulder and matched his steps to the truck. She reached for her door, but he beat her to it with his citrusy scent drawing her to him.

She'd always loved his cologne. Had helped him pick it out over a decade ago. Interesting that he still wore it.

She grabbed the handle above the window. Of course his truck was one of those high-rise kinds, and she was wearing a dress and wedges, making climbing in gracefully nearly impossible. But before she hoisted a foot onto the running board, he extended a hand.

She looked at him.

"I don't bite."

Face heating, she accepted his offer. "Thank you." His callused skin felt rough against hers. She placed her purse on the floorboard and settled into the seat. She waited with hands clasped in her lap for him to get in.

He did and cranked the engine. "How's the little one this morning?"

It touched her that he'd think about Ava. "Rambunctious as ever. We spent the morning playing ring-around-the-rosy." It'd become her favorite game, since Sunday. Trinity Faith's nursery volunteers must've taught it to her.

"You're such a good mom."

Paige's heart squeezed. "Thanks."

"Grandma said how much your mother's enjoyed having the both of you around."

Paige gazed toward the house. She should've brought Ava around more. How sad that it took losing her job to do so.

Jed backed out of the driveway. "Where is this little jewel?"

"Out a ways. Toward Driftwood."

"We'll have plenty of time to get reacquainted, then."

Her stomach did a little flip. She searched her brain for something intelligent to say. Anything besides staring out the window like a lovestruck idiot, which she absolutely wasn't and refused to be.

Besides, he was her boss now, as strange as that felt. What would that be like, working for him? With him? Near him?

Every day.

If the last time they'd spent any consistent time together was any indication, her emotional resolve was one boyish grin away from crumbling.

What then? Could things between them turn out differently this time? But she'd have to stay in Sage Creek. Was she willing to do that?

He turned down a long country road. "My grandma says you've been trying to sell some journalism pieces."

"How would she know—"

"Your mama and her do a lot of talking. Probably more than they should." He laughed. "Makes me wonder what you've been hearing about me."

"I'll never tell." Because she had nothing to tell—nothing but good. He'd refinanced his home, located on fifteen acres about five miles north of town, to save his grandmother's house and business. Spent a good chunk of each week at her place, helping her with lawn care, grocery shopping and whatever else she needed. Went to church every Sunday. The guy was practically perfect.

Who'd ditched his girlfriend for parties and cheerleaders. Maybe if she reminded herself of that often enough, her ricocheting pulse would simmer down.

He passed a slow-moving Chevy. "What got you into fashion?"

She shrugged. "I discovered cute strappy sandals and sequin clutches."

"You still like fishing?"

"Haven't been in a while." Not since the last time Jed took her. Neither of them had caught a thing. Three hours in, a storm had hit and sent them running, shivering and laughing to his truck. They had pulled into a roadside diner, fifteen miles north, for hot cocoa and fries.

"Guess we've got to fix that, don't we?"

She stared at him for a long moment. "What are you doing?"

A tendon in his jaw twitched. "How long you gonna stoke that anger of yours?"

"I'm not. I just… Let's not complicate things, all right?" Every interaction with him initiated questions she didn't have answers to. One in particular she might never know definitively: If she trusted Jed Gilbertson with her heart, would she come to regret it?

"We were real good friends once. Don't make sense to let a hard year destroy what took a lifetime to build."

"Please, Jed. Let's not do this. Not today."

"We need to talk things out sometime. Considering

we're going to be stuck in this truck with one another for a chunk of time, today's as good a day as any."

"Why are you pushing so hard?"

"Because I care for you, woman." He slammed a fist against the steering wheel, making her jump.

She wiped her sweaty palms on her thighs and took in a long, slow breath. "Guess you should've thought of that before you traded me in for Little Miss Pom-Pom."

"Thinking a thing don't make it so."

"What's that supposed to mean?"

His features softened. "I didn't leave you for Christy, and I for sure never cheated on you. I started hanging out with her gang, sure. The other football players, I mean."

A group who'd always snubbed Paige and made her feel like a frizzy-haired outsider. Maybe that was why she became so passionate about fashion. Because in Chicago, at *Chic Fashions* magazine, she'd finally been part of the "in crowd."

Until they'd tossed her out, too.

"But mainly I just chased after the next party. So I didn't have to think about what college I was going to go to, if I'd make it as an adult or how much my father hated me." He scrubbed a hand over his face. "I knew Christy had a thing for me—I'm not going to lie. No, I take that back. She liked that I was a quarterback. And I was flattered."

"Oh, you were a whole lot more than flattered."

"All that talk about us—it was nothing but lies started by her small-minded friends. I never paid her any attention."

"That's not how things looked from where I was standing."

"I listened to her. Laughed at her jokes, maybe. Went to the same parties she did. That was it. I only had eyes for you. I tried telling you that, but you wouldn't listen."

"I don't want to talk about this anymore." Her heart said he was telling the truth. He'd never been the cheating kind. But admitting that would force her to confront her primary reason for pushing him away—fear. Fear of falling in too deeply and allowing her emotions to override her reason, like what had happened with her ex-husband. Fear of choosing Jed and Sage Creek over her independence and career only to find herself heartbroken and unemployed—again.

She'd only truly loved three men in her life—her father, Jed Gilbertson and her ex.

She'd lost all three.

He released a sigh. "Not everyone's like your dad, Paige."

Jed frowned and focused on the long dusty road ahead of him. Why'd he have to push things? Just when Paige was starting to loosen up, even crack a smile on occasion. Now she sat stiffly with her arms crossed, staring out her window. Not saying anything except to bite out which direction to turn.

Great way to start their working relationship.

Should he attempt small talk? Ask about her writing? Nah. Wisest thing he could do was let her simmer down some, chew on what he'd said. But they still had some talking to do—about script-writing stuff. Probably should've stuck with that from the get-go.

"Turn here." She pointed to a dirt road flanked by two long rows of oak trees.

He complied, and they continued down a long, curved road lined with evergreens and splashes of bottlebrush flowers. Dust swirled behind him as pebbles pinged his undercarriage.

They rounded the bend, and a yellow scalloped ranch

with a metal roof and covered porch came into view. The place could use a good paint job, and more dandelions than grass covered the overgrown lawn extending behind it. Not surprising, considering the ministry most likely ran on volunteers and donations.

"Guess this is it." He cut the engine.

She nodded and got out.

He followed her up a lopsided set of stairs.

She rang the bell. "I called this morning and told them we were coming."

"Appreciate it." He hooked a thumb through his belt loop and gazed out at the rolling hills to his right. About five hundred feet past a dilapidated wooden fence stood a partially demolished barn. Wooden planks were stacked nearby.

Paige rang the bell again.

"Coming," a deep voice called out from inside. Heavy footsteps approached, and the door screeched open. "Hey-lo, Paige." A tall man with blond hair curling up from beneath a sweat-stained ball cap grinned at her.

Her countenance instantly softened. "Hey, Noah, thanks for agreeing to see us on such short notice."

"My pleasure." His gaze shifted to Jed. "You must be Mr. Gilbertson."

Jed nodded, and the two shook hands.

"Come in." Noah stepped back. "I'm the founder of New Life Furnishings, a ministry that helps men rebuild their lives through good old-fashioned woodworking. We give a man something productive to do with his hands, something he can be proud of, and something to shoot for." He led them down a long hallway, past a makeshift office and through a galley kitchen. "Don't know how much Paige told you—"

"Just the basics, and the fact that you all have some

quality one-of-a-kind pieces." Despite her detailed descriptions, they were hard to visualize without seeing them for himself. Seemed every time she talked, his mind snagged on something else—like the way her eyes danced when she laughed. Or the adorable way she fiddled with her curls when deep in thought. Or how she rubbed at her collarbone when trying to make a decision.

And the way her entire face lit up whenever Ava came near.

She used to look at him in much the same way, as if he were the only one around.

Noah led them out of the house and down a wooden plank spanning a mud puddle. "Like I said, we do all our work in the old barn out back."

How much had Jed missed? Reining in his thoughts and emotions, he focused on the man's words rather than the beautiful, fiery woman half a step ahead of him.

They followed Noah into a large red barn that had been converted to a woodworking facility, which smelled like cedar and varnish. A handful of men stood over various machines with sawdust swirling around them. Rustic chairs, barstools, tables and bed frames filled one corner, at least ten feet out. Shelves lining the walls about six feet up were filled with prepped branches, stumps, bins of nails and what have you.

Noah sat behind a card table and motioned for Jed and Paige to take seats in front of it. "Chairs and tables, right?"

Jed nodded and explained his needs.

Noah let out a low whistle and repositioned his ball cap. "That's a tall order."

Creases formed across Paige's delicate brow. "How many do you have on hand?"

"Not sure." He moved a thick black binder closer and flipped through it.

She offered Jed a hopeful smile that spiked his pulse. And made him reluctant to look away. Man, was she pretty, and sweeter than Grandma's blackberry pie when she wanted to be. If only he could find a way to coax the sugar from her more often.

"Everything we make here's rustic, simple. A lot of it from reclaimed wood we get right off our land or properties nearby."

The barn Jed saw earlier. Now there was an idea. He knew at least half a dozen farmers and ranchers with rotting structures taking up pasture space. They'd be happy to let Jed and his buddies cart the wood away. He'd get more than enough to panel his theater and then some.

Paige nudged him with her elbow, and he startled. "Huh?"

"When do you need it by?" Noah asked.

"Two weeks."

"Whew. That'd be tight. But we sure could use the money." He pulled out a price sheet and handed it over. "Plus any word of mouth you'd shoot our way."

Paige's eyes latched on to his, as if she were on his side, as if they were in this together.

"All right." Noah exhaled with a quick nod. "We'll do it."

"Yay!" Paige sprang to her feet and spun toward Jed with her eyes looking bright. For a moment, he thought she'd hug him, but then she halted. She turned back to Noah. "Thanks so much. We really appreciate this."

"My pleasure."

Once all of the paperwork had been filled out and a delivery date set, Jed and Paige left. And though she tried to fight it, if the upward twitch of her mouth was any indication, her excitement over their meeting had squelched all those back-off vibes she'd sent his way on the drive over.

Now all Jed needed to do was keep the conversation light for the ride home.

He helped her into his truck and then climbed in beside her. "Got to say, first day on the job, you really knocked it out of the park."

"Thanks," she said, smiling as she put on her seat belt. "Listen, I'm sorry I…acted so sour earlier. I just…" She sighed. "It's just weird, that's all."

"What? Us working together?"

"You being my boss, you mean? Yeah." She gave a soft chuckle and then sobered. "I get what you're trying to do, but—"

"What's that?"

"Resolve things. Act all friendly."

"Is that a crime?"

"This arrangement will be…complicated. Let's not make things any more uncomfortable than they already are."

In other words, back off.

But considering his feelings for her right now, he wasn't sure he could do that.

Chapter Ten

Jed slowed as he neared his grandmother's place. Next door, Paige knelt in front of her mother's flower bed with her back to him. Ava sat beside her, patting the ground with a small shovel—imitating her mom. Seeing the two together struck something paternal and protective in him. Drew him to Paige more than ever.

She'd grown into a strong woman of integrity. An attentive and caring mother. Patient and engaged.

The early afternoon sun accentuated the strawberry blond highlights in her hair. Even from behind, she was beautiful.

He needed to quit thinking like that. It'd only make it harder to keep the employer-employee lines intact between them. And if he stepped even a little over the clear and firm boundaries she'd set repeatedly, he was likely to spook her off for good.

He wanted to talk with her, see if she had any questions regarding the script. He needed to give her the old ones and his drama sketches, so she had something to work with. Problem was, he'd left everything back at the office.

He'd bring them later. In the meantime, he could offer some brainstorming suggestions.

He parked, leaving his engine humming, and got out. Walking toward her, he adjusted his hat.

She must've heard him coming, because she glanced over her shoulder and then stood.

He touched the brim of his Stetson with a short nod. "Paige."

"Hi." She plucked off her gardening gloves. "What can I do for you?"

Used to be, she thought nothing of him stopping by to talk. She'd done the same, often heading over to Grandma's first thing Saturday morning or after school. And not just to see Grandma.

"Hey there, princess." He smoothed a hand over Ava's head, and she studied him with a furrowed brow similar to the one her mother wore. As if both were debating his decency. "Yard's looking good."

"Thanks."

"Glad your mama didn't get lawn fungus like my grandma did. That stuff's a pain."

She shielded her eyes from the sun. "Did she get it taken care of?"

"We're working on it."

A brief silence stretched between them as he racked his brain for something else to say, preferably something witty.

"So, um…" She swiped a lone curl off her forehead. "Can I help you with something?"

He shifted. "Uh…yeah. I was stopping by to see if you'd had a chance to look at the notes I emailed you."

She nodded. "I've been doing some research. I don't know a lot about old train heists."

"I'm not married to the idea, if you have something better."

"I appreciate that." She grabbed a water bottle near

her feet and took a swig. Ava fussed and reached out with her pudgy hands. Paige's face softened to a smile, and she handed her bottle over. Her firm expression returned when her gaze shifted to Jed. "I did stumble upon a Bonnie and Clyde article I found interesting."

"Hmm... You figuring we should do a historical gig, then?"

"I don't know, though it's not a terrible idea. I was talking more about the overall theme—a pair of robbers in love. It could be funny, and romance sells."

He scratched his jaw. Could work. He'd always liked action stories himself, but it was worth a try. Seemed to him any genre would work so long as they put on a good show. And with her doing the writing, it'd give him a glimpse into what touched her heart.

"Sounds like you've given this some thought."

She shrugged. "Like I said, I've barely started researching." Ava dug through the dirt and started throwing it in the air. Paige shook her head. "Uh-uh." She dusted the child's hands off, then scooped her up and gave her a squeeze. "I just received your notes yesterday, remember?"

"Right." He almost chuckled at the stubborn set of her jaw, which made her look as if she were challenging him. Paige had always been competitive. That was what had drawn him—that and the fact she wasn't scared of dirt and mud. And her laugh, man. When she allowed it to come out, it was enough to lasso a fella good.

When was the last time she'd had herself a good laugh?

She brushed dirt from Ava's cheek. "Shall I flesh out my ideas more, then send you a synopsis?"

"A what?"

"A description of the plot."

"Sure. Then maybe we can chat about it."

She nodded. "Call me whenever."

In other words, not in person. Girl wouldn't budge from that "do not cross" boundary she'd created. "I meant to bring you some of our old scripts, so you could see the format, but I plumb forgot."

His phone rang. "Excuse me." He answered. "Hey, Mom. How's your day going?"

"My basement's flooding. Water's everywhere, and your father's out of town. Again." She sounded on the verge of hysterics.

This phone call could take a while. No sense making Paige wait on him. He caught her eye. "I'll catch you later? And I'll bring you those scripts I told you about."

Mom's hysterics stopped. "Who're you talking to?"

He headed toward his truck. "Paige."

A pause. "The Cordell girl?"

"Uh-huh."

"She's back in town?"

He bristled at the edge in her tone. That and past experience told him this was one discussion he'd do well to steer clear of. "Regarding your basement—you call a plumber?"

She huffed. "They don't answer their phone. Meanwhile my leather furniture is sitting in a pond of water. Pretty soon my wood floors will start warping."

He climbed into his truck, still watching Paige. Would've been nice to continue their conversation some—might've even invited her to coffee.

Then what? Would she stay in Sage Creek? If she did, could they start dating again? They hadn't done so well the last time they'd tried. True, life had been hard and chaotic, but that was practically always the case.

And what about sweet little Ava? Was Jed ready to

be a father? He couldn't pursue Paige until he knew, for certain, the answer to that question was yes.

"Jed Gilbertson, are you listening to me?"

He startled at his mother's sharp reprimand. "Sorry, Mom. What were you saying?"

"Your mind's on that girl again, isn't it? Seriously, Jed, didn't you learn the first time? Paige Cordell isn't—"

"Can you shut the water off?" He pulled into the street, casting one last glance at Paige.

She stood, positioning Ava on her hip. She looked his way, and his heart did a loop-the-loop.

He looked away and focused his wayward brain cells back on his phone conversation.

"How?" She sounded on the verge of tears. "It's coming from the water heater or whatever that cylinder-like thing is in the storage room."

He wasn't sure where the shut-off valve might be. "Sit tight. I'm on my way."

"Thanks, sweetie. I don't know what I'd do without you."

"No biggie." He headed toward the house he'd spent the first eighteen years of his life in and called Grandma on the way.

"Hello?"

"Hey-yah. I'm out and about and wanted to make sure you didn't need anything."

"Not that I can think of. Where you headed?"

"Mom's." He relayed the information of the water situation.

"Oh, my." She paused. "Is there anything I can do?"

"Not that I can think of, unless you've got a skilled plumber on speed dial."

"I wouldn't know anyone she hasn't already called. Tell her hello for me?"

"Will do."

"Think she'd join us for church Sunday?"

Unlikely, but Grandma had to know that already, considering all of her invites over the years had been declined. "I'll ask."

"That's all you can do."

"True enough. You busy Saturday morning?"

"Besides cleaning out my freezer? Nope."

"How about making culinary inventions with me?"

"For the dinner theater?"

"Yep. Figure we'll need a new menu, home-on-the-range style, to go with our new decor."

"That fancy chef we pay so much won't come up with something?"

"Might if we force him." But the guy didn't have a creative bone in his stiff-necked body, and the mere suggestion of change made him balk.

"Saturday sounds fun. You should invite Paige to join us. She always loved fiddling in the kitchen."

She wouldn't be interested if she knew Jed would be there. "I best get going. You have a good day, and watch yourself doing yard work. It's supposed to be a scorcher."

"So I hear, though that doesn't seem to stop that pretty new neighbor of ours none. I swear she's been out there weeding her mama's flower beds for going on an hour."

He'd seen.

"What a sweet thing she is, helping Marilyn like she does, and with a little one underfoot. A smart fella would snatch that girl right up."

"Grandma." This wasn't something he wanted to talk about.

He ended the call. He mulled over every conversation he'd had with Paige since she'd returned to town. Every conversation he'd had with her, period, until his thoughts were a jumble of things past, present and future.

By the time he made it to Mom's basement, she'd pulled up the area rugs and had laid numerous towels and linens across the floor.

Face flushed, she swiped the back of her hand against her sweat-glistened forehead. "Finally got a plumber to return my call. Said he'd be here first thing tomorrow." She threw up her hands. "What am I supposed to do till then?"

"Give me a sec to turn off the water." He checked the water heater and sump pump first. Wasn't there. He stepped gingerly through the growing puddle, toward a small walk-in behind the gym. "Found it." He shut off the valve, then set to work mopping up the pond seeping into his mother's wood floor. Next he set portable fans and space heaters on dry surfaces throughout the room.

"Thanks, sweetie." She started to hug him, glanced at his wet shirt, then smiled and patted his cheek. But then she frowned.

"What? Something wrong?"

"I didn't realize you were hanging out with the Cordell girl again."

Arguing with Mom would only work her up more. "She works for me."

"What do you mean?"

He explained the situation, intentionally leaving out the part about her getting fired from her job in Chicago. "Why do you hate her so much anyway?"

"I don't hate her. I just have my concerns. We've talked about this."

Fourteen years ago. Mom had been wrong about Paige then, and she was doubly wrong about her now. Hopefully, given time, she'd come to see that. Regardless, he wasn't interested in resurrecting a decade-old argument, especially not when his mom was stressed and standing in a flooded basement.

He stepped toward the sliding glass door. "I've got to go." If he stayed much longer, he'd say something he'd regret. "Call if you need me."

For now that was how their conversation regarding Paige needed to end. Though it wasn't a discussion he could continue to avoid, not if things progressed between them.

His mom had said often enough that if a man dated a girl, he dated her whole family. Well, the converse was true as well, and even more so when a man and woman got married. If he was going to even consider making Paige a Gilbertson, he needed to make sure that'd be a welcoming, joy-filled transition.

For both her and sweet little Ava.

Chapter Eleven

Paige glanced at her daily planner and sighed. She'd blocked out Ava's nap time to work on the dinner-theater script, but had no idea how to get started. And her long list of ideas weren't helping. Maybe Jed had given her too much leeway.

He was supposed to drop material off yesterday, but said he'd gotten hung up at his mom's. Did that indicate a lack of follow-through? If so, working for him would be rough.

Rough*er*.

She hated wasting time and writing under unrealistically tight deadlines. That only made failure more inevitable. She glanced through the window, at the cloud cover blanketing the skyline, suggesting dramatically cooler temperatures. Maybe she should shift her run, which she'd planned to go on this evening, to earlier. She grabbed her eraser and made the changes, scheduling in script writing for after supper.

So long as Jed showed up. It was almost ironic, considering how much time she'd spent trying to avoid him, that now she was anxious for him to arrive.

Only for the script samples.

And maybe if she told herself that enough times, her rebellious heart would believe it.

She thought back to their conversation the day they drove to New Life Furnishings. Thought back to their senior year in high school, when Jed had joined the football team and started hanging out with the jocks and pompoms crowd. He'd said he hadn't left her for Christy, but they had dated…eventually. The question was when did they officially get together? Had Paige pushed Jed in that direction with her accusations?

What might have happened if she'd listened to him that day, when he'd tried to talk to her, to deny the rumors and profess his love? What if she had believed him?

She never would've met her ex-husband. Wouldn't be divorced now.

Nor would she have had precious little Ava.

Something one of her old Sunday-school teachers used to say swept through her mind. *God can bring out good, even in the hard.*

Her phone pinged an incoming email. It was from her uncle. She opened it, skimmed it and laughed. In response to her writer's block comment, shared in a message she sent him this morning, he'd listed at least fifty random, nonsensical ideas. Murder over Maggie's magnificent magnolias. A sweet tooth savagely seeks out cookies. Mayhem at the Texas State Fair's cake baking competition—because chocolate can be deadly.

"All perfect," she replied.

Mom was in her bedroom, napping off a headache. Paige sent her a text to keep an ear out for Ava, changed into her running gear and then left.

The air was muggier than she'd anticipated, and soon sweat trickled down her temples and between her shoulder blades. Even so, it felt good to stretch her legs and give her mind time to decompress. The writers' conference was approaching quickly, and she was beginning to have doubts about going. Should she trust Ava with Mom for two overnights? She'd been attentive and engaged, but quick to retreat.

Maybe Mrs. Tappen could help keep an eye out?

The bigger question—what made Paige think she'd land another writing job, one that paid enough to cover the expense of living in the city? Besides, there'd be hundreds, probably thousands, of other writers at the conference, all vying for positions.

What if Paige hadn't been let go simply because of budget cuts? What if she'd stunk at her job? Her stomach knotted.

So she'd start at the bottom, doing grunt work, fact-checking, whatever she could find to get her foot in the door somewhere.

But was it worth it? Leaving Sage Creek, Mom, Mira, Mrs. Tappen…

Jed.

Was Jed worth staying for?

Pounding out her confusion and uncertainty with every step, she zigzagged her way to the jogging trail marking the circumference of Mirror Lake.

Four laps in, the wind picked up, and the sky darkened as thick rain clouds swept in. It looked as though she were about to get—

A fat raindrop plopped onto her forehead. *Wet.*

Another followed, and then another. Lightning flashed, unleashing a torrent that soon sent goose pimples up her arm. By the time she made it home, she was drenched. Her hair and clothes clung to her, and mud splattered her calves and shins.

She opened the front door and poked her head inside. "Mom, can you bring me a towel?" she called out.

Nothing.

"Mom?" She stomped her feet and stepped inside.

She shivered and headed toward Mom's bedroom. "You awake?"

She sighed and started to turn toward the hall bathroom when the guest bedroom's door creaked open.

"What's gotten…" Mom's eyes widened, and then a grin formed on her face. "Girl, you're a mess. What'd you do, fall into a crick?"

"It's raining. Ava still asleep?"

"Like a rock." Mom closed the bedroom door softly behind her. "Wait there and I'll grab you a towel."

The doorbell rang, and Paige stiffened. *Jed?* Of all of the times for him to finally show up…

Mom stopped midway to the bathroom. "You going to get that?" Before she could answer, Mom returned, reached around her and opened the door. "Jed, hello. Come in."

"Mrs. Cordell. Paige." With a tip of his Stetson, he offered a soft smile, and the tenderness in his eyes captivated her.

She pushed her soggy hair out of her face. "Hi."

He set an umbrella near the door and then stepped inside. His gaze swept the length of her with a hint of a smile on his lips. "Looks like you got yourself caught in the storm." He held papers wrapped inside a plastic grocery bag.

"Something like that." She swiped at the mascara streaks she knew shadowed her eyes. "Give me a minute?"

"Of course."

As she dashed into the bathroom for a towel, Mom

ushered Jed into the living room with an offer of biscuits and sweet tea.

Paige gripped the sink and stared at her blotchy reflection in the mirror. Jed always seemed to show up at the most inopportune times. First after her grueling two-day drive from Chicago. Then when she'd rushed outside the following Saturday, in her pajamas. Her dumpster-diving endeavor. Now this.

He probably thought she was a scattered, soggy mess.

Except, the way he looked at her, whether put together or with unkempt, frizzy hair, said differently. Suggested he loved her.

Dare she believe that? And even if it were true, was he prepared for what that meant?

Was he ready to be a dad, to hold tightly not just to her, but to Ava, as well?

She yanked a towel off the rack, squeezed it around her hair and rubbed the smudges beneath her eyes. She turned on the faucet and gave her face a good wash, causing her sensitive skin to flare bright red. Lovely.

She hurried to her room to exchange her wet clothing for jeans and a T-shirt. Ava lay curled on her side, sucking her thumb. After a night of fussing, a long nap would do her good.

Paige softly kissed her cheek. "My precious girl." She'd do anything in her power to ensure her daughter always looked so happy and content. To keep her free from pain.

Pulling her hair into a ponytail, she sucked in a deep breath, and joined Mom and Jed in the living room.

He placed his mug on the end table and stood. "Sorry I didn't make it over earlier. It's been one of those days."

"No problem."

Mom pushed to her feet. "If you'll excuse me, I better…" She glanced at her computer, then about the room. "I have things to attend to." She shot Paige a wink before shuffling off to her bedroom.

Subtle, Mom. What was this, high school? Sometimes, like now, it felt like it. She turned to Jed with what she hoped was a professional smile, ignoring the tingle that swept through her when his deep chocolate eyes snagged hers. After all of these years, he could still initiate an intense reaction within her.

Did he feel the same?

Did she want him to?

"These the old scripts?" She motioned toward a stack of papers on the coffee table.

He nodded and handed them over. "I brought the one we're using now, though I have to warn you, it's pretty bad." He offered a sheepish smile. "There's also seven or so we've used in the past, which aren't that much better. Some of these are pretty old. Found them in a filing cabinet in my office when I came on board."

She sat, and he did the same with his leg brushing against hers and sending a rush of warmth through her. Clearing her throat, she inched aside to add distance between them and grabbed the first drama on his pile. It was covered in red where someone had crossed things off, circled parts and jotted notes in the margin.

"That's what we're using now." He leaned closer to read over her shoulder. His breath smelled like peppermint. "It called for too many cast members."

"I see." She turned the page, noting clues highlighted in yellow. "How many clues do you normally have per script?"

"A dozen, give or take—some intentionally false."

"Red herrings?"

His forehead creased. "What?"

"Mystery-writing lingo."

He grinned. "I figured you'd know your stuff."

"A little. Does your cast always have three males and four females?"

"Thereabouts. More than that, and things get jumbled. 'Course, if you think you can write something with a crew of six or less, even better. We've got to cut costs where we can." His crooked smile stalled her breath.

Triggering emotions she'd thought she'd long abandoned. Emotions that had the potential to change everything, if she let them.

Jed deposited five grocery bags on his grandmother's kitchen table.

"Boy, what have I let you talk me into?" Mirth filled her eyes. "How much cooking were you thinking we'd do?"

"We need at least five signature dishes with one unique enough to get some press. Maybe a soup and appetizer, too."

"By *unique* you don't mean something nasty like deep-fried cow hearts, I hope."

"Hmm…hadn't thought of that one, but it'd be unexpected, for sure."

"And uneaten."

He laughed and pulled some old cookbooks he'd purchased at the used bookstore from one of his bags. "I did find a recipe for pickled cowboy candy, though." He flipped to the dog-eared page. "I'd want to tweak it some."

"Like how? Dip the jalapenos in chocolate?"

"Not hardly." He started unloading groceries onto the counter. "Though that might be better than chocolate-covered crickets."

She flipped through marked recipes and suggested palatable changes, while Jed took notes. By early afternoon, they'd come up with four possible main dishes and a dessert he titled Rancher's Bark. Its dark chocolate base was embedded with toffee chunks, chopped macadamia nuts and bits of bacon, all topped with caramel drizzles.

Jed decided to tackle cleanup—so he could lick the bowl. He ran the spatula along the chocolate-covered porcelain, careful to pick up as many bacon bits as possible, and then savored its salty sweetness.

"Don't know where you put all that." Grandma surveyed their creations, lined in plastic storage containers on nearly every available surface space. "Hope you'll take most of this home with you."

He placed a hand over his over-full stomach and groaned. "I've had enough to last me a week." He'd tried each dish, eating more of some than others.

"You know—" she grabbed a paper bag from the pantry "—I wonder if our sweet neighbors would enjoy trying our concoctions."

A jolt ran through him, initiating a grin before he could halt it. He quickly covered with a cough. "Sure. I could bring a dish or two over to their house."

Grandma's lips twitched toward a smile. "Paige sure has turned mighty pretty."

He stepped toward the counter before Grandma could see the blush taking over his face. "She's all right." Beautiful, feisty and stubborn with enough brilliance and creativity to salvage their dying business.

And steal his heart, if he let her.

He would, too, if he thought that was what she wanted.

"Might as well take a few dishes over now." He grabbed the Texas Hash made with quail and shredded sweet potatoes.

"You do that." Her teasing tone made him bristle.

If only Paige wasn't dead set on returning to Chicago.

He paused at Grandma's door to slip on his Stetson and cowboy boots, and then he made his way over to Mrs. Cordell's. Funny how his insides felt all jittery, kind of like that first day, many years ago, when he'd asked her out.

If he had it to do over…

He rotated his shoulders, stretched his neck from side to side and reached for the doorbell.

Mrs. Cordell answered before he got a chance to ring. She smelled like a mixture of lavender and something spicy he couldn't place. "Jed, hello. Please come in."

He obliged and glanced about. "Is Paige here?" He clamped his mouth shut, wishing he'd given his brain half a second to catch up with his tongue. "What I mean is…" He thrust his container of food at her. "I brought this over. I'll probably add it to our menu and figured she—and you—might want a preview taste."

She took the hash with the same knowing expression Grandma had given him. "How thoughtful. If you don't mind waiting… She's trying to get Ava down to sleep. The munchkin's been fighting her, the little crab apple. Most likely letting her know just how displeased she was at having her mama gone most of the day."

"Oh?"

"She went to a job fair or some such thing."

So Paige was still job hunting. For something in Sage Creek? Did that mean she planned to stay?

His heart surged at the thought.

Man, was he in trouble.

Chapter Twelve

Paige held Ava tightly in her arms with her chin rested on top of her curly head. She continued rocking, though the child's steady breathing indicated she'd fallen asleep at least ten minutes ago. These were the moments Paige cherished. And tonight they helped brighten what had otherwise been a discouraging day.

The career fair had been a waste of time. Of the dozen or so companies she'd encountered, most were looking for secretaries or salespeople. Not that it made any sense for her to go, considering she had no intention of staying in Sage Creek any longer than necessary.

But she was beginning to get desperate. Her savings were dwindling, and the few articles she'd sold had only earned her half a car payment.

Her every hope rode on the writers' conference and finding a steady, well-paying writing gig, if not for a magazine, then maybe for a nonprofit or something. With ten magazines and nearly an equal number of advocacy-related organizations represented, she had to land something.

This kind of thinking only added to her stress level and did nothing to silence her anxiety.

And thoughts of Jed Gilbertson.

Of his smile, the little things he said, the way he looked at her. Looked at Ava.

And how much he and Mrs. Tappen were counting on her to write a phenomenal script.

She was still trying to wrap her thoughts around the whole process. Emcee intro, audience participation, at least one cast member hidden among the paying attendees. It felt like a steep learning curve, one that sapped every last drop of her creativity.

All on a locomotive, if she wrote out Jed's train-heist premise. He'd said to let him know if she had a better idea, which she didn't.

"Sleep well, sweet girl." Paige tucked Ava beneath the covers, kissed her forehead and started to slip out.

Voices from the kitchen halted her.

Jed was here?

A flutter swept through her gut, and she paused to catch a glimpse of her reflection in the wall mirror. For once, her hair actually looked good, and she'd opted for her regular clothes over bleach-stained yoga pants this morning.

With a deep breath and a quick fluff to her curls, she exited the room and softly closed the door behind her.

"Howdy." Jed stepped out from the kitchen with her mom following close behind.

"Uh… Hi." She set her bag on the ground near the wall. "I didn't hear the door."

"I saw him from the window as he was walking up." Mom smiled. "Caught him before he rang the bell. Didn't want him making a ruckus while you were putting Ava down."

"I appreciate that." She eyed Jed. "So… What's up?"

"I came bearing gifts." His grin made her feel askew. "The edible kind."

She raised an eyebrow. "All right. So, what'd you bring?"

"Supper."

"And it's good," Mom said. "Settling to my upset stomach—it's been giving me fits today. I put a call in to my doctor, left a message on the nurse's line." She went on to talk about an article she'd read about hiatal hernias and why she felt certain she had one.

Paige cleared her throat to divert the conversation. "When'd you turn into a chef?" She couldn't image Jed voluntarily stepping behind a stove.

Actually, she could, and she found the image much too endearing.

"Not sure I'd go that far. I showed up with the ideas, ingredients and a bunch of recipes to serve as inspiration. Then I alternated between following directions and staying out of Grandma's way while she worked her magic."

Sweet old Mrs. Tappen. She could make most anything edible.

"You two chat while I serve up a couple plates." Mom returned to the kitchen, leaving Paige alone in the living room with Jed. A predicament that could prove dangerous.

She'd returned to Sage Creek to regroup, not fall in love.

"I'll help." She followed Mom, and heard Jed's heavy footfalls close behind. While Mom pulled plates from the cupboard, Paige darted to the fridge.

"It's on the top shelf." Jed pointed. "In the container with the pink lid."

She pulled the food out. It didn't look all that appetizing, but it smelled amazing. "Might want to tweak the presentation some, if you plan to serve it." Her stomach growled loudly, causing Jed to chuckle and her face to flame.

"Yeah. Grandma's going to work on that."

Once she'd heated two platefuls, she handed one to him and brought hers to the living room, taking Mom's seat behind her desk.

Jed sat on the couch, catty-corner to Mom in her recliner. "Didn't think I'd be able to eat another bite, after all the tasting I did this afternoon, but man alive..." He shook his head and scooped a forkful of cheesy goo. "This stuff is good."

She inhaled the garlicky bacon scent and dipped her spoon into the mixture. "What's in this?" She took a bite, then closed her eyes as pure heaven exploded on her tongue. Sweet, salty and creamy with a slight crunch.

He set his fork on his plate. "Don't go trying to get me to share Grandma's secrets. She might start banning me from her kitchen."

Paige smiled. "What a shame that'd be."

He rubbed his stomach. "That right there could send a man into withdrawal. So, tell me about this career fair. Any leads?"

She glanced at Mom, who looked so peaceful, almost happy, sitting in her recliner. No sense souring her mood with a reminder of Paige's eventual departure. "Not really. Not anything I'm qualified for or interested in."

"Guess that means you won't be bailing on Grandma and I anytime soon, then, huh?" Though his words suggested he spoke in jest, the intensity in his eyes caused her breath to stutter.

"Don't worry—I have every intention of completing the terms of our contract."

"And when that's over, who knows, right?" Mom gave

a nervous laugh, then sobered. "It's been nice having you here, Paige. Real nice."

Mom's words weighed heavily on her heart. She'd stayed away too long, had been way too detached. Calling her mother on holidays, sending the occasional card. She'd always been in such a rush, so focused on her career, and then surviving her divorce, she'd been so oblivious to Mom's pain.

Paige agreed; it was good she was here, at least for now.

What about Jed? She looked over to find him watching her. Not just observing her, but studying her, as if he were trying to figure her out or something.

He used to do that a lot, when they were in high school. He'd joked that he wanted to memorize her every freckle.

She shook the thought aside and focused on finishing her supper while trying to ignore the handsome, attentive man sitting across from her. Though, he was probably more interested in her opinion of his new menu item.

"This is good." Plate cleaned, she set it down. "If this is any indication of your other entrees, you should draw quite a crowd."

"Especially once we put your script into action."

She frowned and dropped her gaze. He had way too much faith in her. What if her drama was stupid and actually kept people away? Then she'd be a failure twice over. And she'd devastate Mrs. Tappen in the process. She couldn't do that.

Which meant it was time she asked for help. "Listen, the mystery... I'm struggling a little."

"Okay." He leaned forward and placed his elbows on his knees with his hands twined and dangling between them. "How can I help?"

"Well..." How could she explain that every time she

opened her computer screen, her mind went blank? Especially when her thoughts drifted in his direction? "I know we talked about a Bonnie and Clyde plot, but..." She frowned. "If we go that route, I'm afraid the show will be predictable."

"What do you mean?"

"How hard do you think it'll be for your patrons to figure out the crime-spree duo committed the murder?"

"Ah. I see what you mean." He scratched his jaw. "What if they weren't the killers? Maybe they could even be the sleuths. That'd throw people off, right?"

"True. That brings us to motive and backstory."

"Okay."

"Would you mind brainstorming with me?"

"For sure. Where should we start?"

"How about we go to the kitchen?" She stood. "I've got all of my notes in there."

He nodded, and Mom rose with a groan. "Think I'll head in to bed. Rest these aching bones of mine. Do some reading." She crossed the room and kissed Paige's cheek. "Love you, Doodlebug."

Paige smiled at her old childhood nickname. "You, too."

Except, now she'd be alone with Jed. Her stomach flip-flopped. Feigning confidence she far from felt, she raised her chin and took long, brisk steps toward the kitchen. She flicked the light on en route to the table.

Jed sat across from her with his long legs stretched out to the side and his ankles crossed. "Doodlebug." He chuckled. "I'd forgotten that one."

"Whatever, baby boy." It'd only taken the neighborhood kids hearing his grandmother's endearing term once to run with it—not exactly what young boys wanted to

be called. Although that was much better than what some
of the older kids nicknamed him—Jed the Booginator.

But she'd never tease him about that one. No one liked
to remember their experiences with school bullies, even
if Jed had eventually grown up and filled out enough
in high school to silence those jerks. Funny, he'd never
tried to get revenge. As the quarterback with a pack of
muscly friends on his side, he could've easily made his
former tormentors pay.

"What's got that busy little brain of yours turning?"
Tenderness radiated from his eyes.

She straightened. "Huh?"

"What're you thinking about? Based on your frown,
it must be something important."

She studied him. "I was just thinking about the Fuller
twins."

He laughed. "Man, were they troublemakers. I thought
for sure they'd both end up in juvie before their thirteenth
birthday. Although Dalton didn't fare much better. He
landed in prison before he hit twenty."

"Really? For what?"

"Involuntary manslaughter—bar fight that got out of
hand. But the other one, Clayton, he's really turned himself around. Married with a couple of young'uns. He's a
pretty good carpenter—he's helped me knock out a wall
or two. Matter of fact, I should probably give him a call
to see if he can help us with our renovations."

"You're kidding, right?"

"About what? Him knowing how to handle a hammer?
He always did like working with his hands."

"It's hard to believe you'd let him near your theater.
I mean, I get grace and everything, but wow. I couldn't
do that."

"Forgive someone?"

"Forgive maybe, but bless?" She shook her head. "That had to be hard."

"We were a couple of stupid kids, not to mention the Fullers' old man was a mean drunk who beat their mama in front of them."

"I didn't know that." But still, a rough upbringing didn't give anyone license to act like a bully. "So you're saying their daddy made them do it?"

"No. I'm saying I've chosen to let it go." His face softened, and his gaze latched on to hers as if he could see deep into her heart. As if what he saw broke his. "All your anger is tearing you up. You've got to let it go."

How had this conversation taken such a personal turn? "Please, let's not talk about that now."

"I'm here as a friend."

"Don't." She raised her hand and pushed her notebook aside. "It's late, and I'm tired. I think you should leave."

He remained seated, watching her with the kindness in his gaze threatening to push her to tears. But she refused to cry in front of him.

He stood. "I'll see myself out. Have a good night."

As she watched him leave, an ache so deep that it squeezed her lungs spread through her chest.

His grandmother's words, spoken the day they made cinnamon rolls, resurfaced. *What if God brought you here to help you heal?*

And maybe even to love again? Was she brave enough to try?

Chapter Thirteen

Jed closed his office door to mute the renovation noises reverberating through the theater. Total costs looked to be tracking a bit higher than he'd hoped. But maybe if he and his buddies tackled the lobby themselves…

A knock sounded on the opened door, and he glanced up.

Paige stood in the hallway, wearing a cute little sundress that brought out the peach undertones in her skin. She wore the top half of her hair pulled back. The rest cascaded to her shoulders in loose curls with a few tighter ringlets framing her face. A slight pink highlighted her soft shoulders and cheekbones, as if she'd been in the sun.

"Hi." Her voice was soft, and she appeared to be having a tough time maintaining eye contact.

Seemed she grew more beautiful every time he saw her. "Hey." He motioned her in and stood to meet her. "Come in. Everything all right?"

"Yeah, I just… I had some questions about the script… Do you have any reference materials I could borrow?"

"On script writing, you mean?"

"No. History. On trains, heists, robberies in the 1800s? I've found some information and images, what have you, online but was hoping for… I don't know exactly. I figured you probably did a fair amount of research before deciding on the renovations and might have kept some of the books."

He quirked a brow at her. "You asking if I've got a library stashed somewhere?"

She laughed. "Right. I'd almost forgotten your book allergy."

It was nice to know she felt comfortable enough with him again to tease him like this. The girl was beautiful regardless, but when she laughed and her smile lit her eyes… It was enough to make a man lose all sense. "We could visit the Pioneer Museum. I need some decorating ideas anyway."

She studied him, as if she were weighing his words, or maybe trying to place motive behind them. "Mind if I bring Ava along?"

"Of course not." He got a kick out of that little girl, though he knew he couldn't let himself get too attached. She and her mom would be leaving soon enough.

"A museum visit sounds nice. That way I can bounce ideas off you, ask questions or whatever." She paused. "Script writing is new to me. I don't want to mess this up."

Poor girl was as nervous as a foal in a pen of steeds. Had her mom told her how much was at stake? Probably. She'd never been tight with her words. If Paige knew Grandma would lose her home if the theater didn't turn around right quick, she'd be knotted up with fear. He needed to do what he could to reassure her. Build her confidence.

"You got time to go now?" He'd planned on working on payroll this afternoon, but he could do that later. "I could slip away for a few hours."

"Sure. I'll call my mom. Ask her to have Ava ready."

"Great." He sprang to his feet, fighting a grin. *Keep it professional.* This was nothing more than a work-related deal. Hoping for anything else would smack him square on the noggin.

He led the way out and down the hall.

She paused at the front entrance. "I'll see you in a few."

"Makes more sense to drive together, don't you think?"

She scraped her teeth across her bottom lip. "All right." She offered a hint of a smile. "Just let me grab my purse."

A moment later, she met him at his truck, climbed in and sat quietly with her hands clasped in her lap, the way she had on their trip to New Life Furnishings…toward the end. Truth be told, she'd almost turned chatty until he had started blabbing about the past. *Note to self—steer clear of potentially painful or irritating topics.*

He stopped at a four-way. "When you worked for that fashion magazine, what'd you write about?" Lame conversation starter, especially considering his knowledge of fashion consisted of where to buy the cheapest, most durable pair of jeans.

"It varied. I wrote features, so I spent a lot of time with designers."

"That must've been interesting."

"It was."

"Bet you've got some interesting stories to tell."

"Most of the designers were pretty normal, but there was this one woman." Her soft laugh captivated him. "I usually did interviews at restaurants to keep conversations relaxed. But this one designer wanted to meet at a vintage wedding store, which wouldn't have been so bad, but turned out she had a reason for the location."

"Which was?"

"She started trying on dresses. Like nearly every one."

"Why?"

"For the magazine pictures."

"That'd frustrate me to no end. I'm guessing you didn't get much interviewing done."

"It took a while. All day, to be exact."

He pulled into her mom's driveway and put his truck in Park.

"I'll be right back." She dashed out and returned with a grinning Ava on her hip and an overstuffed diaper bag dangling from her shoulder. Her mom followed her out, waved and then hurried to her car. She returned a moment later with Ava's car seat.

"Ma'am." He tipped his hat at her.

"Jed, good to see you."

He helped her get the car seat in, and then he stepped out of the way so Paige could strap her little one in.

"All set, little princess?" He squeezed her foot.

"Me and Mommy bye-bye. To see the pwetty dwesses."

He laughed. "I'm sure there'll be plenty of those." He held a fisted hand out to her, but she just stared at it. "Aw, come on. Don't leave me hanging. Give your buddy Jed a fist bump, now." She continued to stare at him, so he grabbed her little hand, gave it a quick shake and then bopped her nose.

"Guess that means you're good to go." He winked, stepped back and shut her door.

"You all have fun." Humor danced in Mrs. Cordell's eyes, suggesting that she suspected he and her daughter were heading out for more than a research outing.

If only that were true.

Then again, why couldn't it be? He'd captured her heart once. He just needed to do so again—to keep her in Sage Creek for good.

He kept the conversation light on the way to the museum. When Ava attempted to join in, he made sure to include her. That was easy enough, so long as he mentioned horses or puppies. Matter of fact, he got a kick out of just how talkative the little girl was.

After a while, Paige began loosening up, too. By the time he pulled into the museum parking lot, it was almost as if the old Paige had reemerged.

The Paige he'd fallen in love with.

And he couldn't—wouldn't—lose her again.

With Ava in her arms, Paige slowed as she exited the museum's restroom. She watched Jed chat with a pair of kids while their mother stood, laughing, a foot away. Paige vaguely recognized the woman, though whether from her school days, Trinity Faith or having bumped into her around town, she wasn't sure. She couldn't hear what Jed was saying, but she assumed a ridiculous joke was involved.

He'd been in a punny mood today. It had started when she'd shared an idea she had for what she hoped to be a hilarious shoot-out. Playing on the words *quick draw*, and then having the less-than-intelligent bandit go searching for a pencil and paper.

Cheesy, but Jed acted like the whole scenario was the funniest thing since Andy's cow-tipping attempts. He'd spent the rest of the morning either teasing Ava or popping off one joke after another.

Hanging out like this and acting goofy with each other felt like old times. Made her long for what they'd had, before life had knocked her flat and Jed had gotten caught up with the popular group.

But had he left her, or had she been the one to pull

away first? Regardless, he should've held tightly to her. Fought for her.

Like her daddy should've done with Mom, and should've done with her.

Jed's statement, spoken softly yet firmly that day they'd driven to New Life Furnishings, swirled through her mind. *Not everyone's like your dad, Paige.*

The boys Jed had been talking to darted off, and he glanced her way with an adorable tilt of his mouth.

She was falling, too deeply and too quickly.

He sauntered over with one hand in his jeans' pocket. "You ladies hungry?" He poked Ava in the belly, producing a giggle. "What do you say, Miss Curly Q? You aching for some broccoli and onions?"

Ava pushed her bottom lip out and crossed her arms, shaking her head with such enthusiasm, her curls zinged back and forth.

Paige laughed and kissed Ava's cheek.

"What do you say, Mama?" His gaze snagged hers. "Want to grab a bite before we head back?"

"Sure. We could do that." Clearly, her heart, not her head, had control of her mouth. But it was just a meal. With an incredibly handsome man. Whom she'd once loved deeply.

And was beginning to fear that maybe, just maybe, she still did.

"Awesome." He guided her out of the museum with a hand to the small of her back. "Don't know about you, but I'm getting pretty stoked. I've got a lot of decorating ideas."

As they stepped out into the hot noon sun, Jed dropped his hand. She felt an urge to inch closer to him, if only to feel his touch once again.

Stop that! She smoothed her hair behind her ears and

focused on his truck. Anything other than the strong cowboy walking beside her. "Coming here was a great idea. I've got a lot of ideas, too."

"Like what?" At his truck, he unlocked it and then reached past her to open her door. Always the gentleman, he took Ava from her, buckled her in and then rounded the truck to the driver's side.

When he climbed in, she pulled a notebook and pen from her purse. "The first idea's kind of silly, maybe a little too slapstick."

"Slapstick might work. Let's have it."

"You've heard the phrase 'acknowledging the corn'?"

"Yep. Means telling the truth."

"So, during the 'investigation,' the sheriff could say something about folks needing to acknowledge the corn and one of the cast members could grab someone's corn and start chatting it up. Like I said, a little silly—"

"It's all in the setup and delivery."

"I hope to knock out the first draft tonight. Hopefully you and your grandma will like it."

"I'm sure it'll be great. You've always been a fantastic writer."

"But this is new." She ran a hand up and down the back of her arm. "I've never even been to a murder-mystery theater before."

"Really?"

She gave a one-shoulder shrug.

"Guess we best rectify that, then. But my place is out—the remodeling started this morning. We won't have another show until the reopening." He frowned. "Might be hard getting tickets—most other dinner theaters sell out pretty quick." He drummed his fingers on the steering wheel. "Tell you what, I'll do some calling around, see what I can find."

A night out with Jed. Like a date.

That wasn't a date.

She took a slow, deep breath to rein in her emotions.

They were spending way too much time together already.

Ava chattered in the seat behind them. Mostly gibberish, but Paige made out a few words. *House, mama...* and *rabbit*?

Jed laughed and looked back through the rearview mirror. "That's quite a story, princess."

He was better with kids than she would've expected. Kind. Attentive. Hilarious.

Much better than her baby-leaving ex-husband.

She'd lose a lot if she moved back to Chicago, and not just whatever might come of her and Jed. She'd lose their friendship, too, which, if she were being honest, she'd really missed. They'd been so close once.

But she'd be giving up a lot, risking a lot, to stay.

They arrived at Wilma's to find the lunch crowd had already come and gone, which only added to Paige's awkwardness. The quiet demanded to be filled with more than Ava's constant chatter. Though, her prattle did help. It kept Jed occupied and the conversation centered on safe topics, such as children's songs, random animals and the abundance of toys Paige kept stocked in her diaper bag.

But then the waitress brought their food and Ava became preoccupied with finger painting her tray with peanut butter and jelly.

Jed leaned forward with his mocha eyes latched on to hers. "I had a nice time today."

She swallowed. "I did, too." Too nice. She thought back to the first time he'd taken her to Wilma's. It had been two weeks after their first kiss. Two long, silent weeks where, whenever he saw her, he'd duck his head and dart away.

She'd become convinced he didn't like her, that the kiss had been a mistake, or maybe he'd acted on a dare. But then, one Friday, she'd arrived at her school locker to find him waiting, looking adorably shy, wanting to know if she wanted to grab something to eat.

She'd almost squealed her answer, but then, with a slow, deep breath had nodded and said, as nonchalantly as her squeaky voice allowed, "That'd be fun."

"What're you thinking about?"

"Huh?" Her face heated.

"You've got that dreamy, 'I'm plotting a murder' expression going on. You figure out another false clue?"

"Red herring."

"Yeah, that."

"I was just..." *Reminiscing on the best year of my life. Followed by the worst year.*

Chapter Fourteen

Jed swiveled his desk chair to face his computer and started skimming through his emails. Most were spam. A couple of script-writing companies had responded to his questions with sample pages, and one was following up regarding material they'd sent a month back. They weren't the kind he'd use—too crude.

Good thing he had Paige. He smiled, thinking back to their afternoon at the museum. For a few precious hours, the old Paige had emerged—and stayed. And like he'd hoped, perusing exhibits had stirred her imagination. By the time they'd left, she'd been bubbling with plot ideas.

She was talented enough to write the thing on her own, but apparently she was still too uncertain to do so.

Or did she just enjoy spending time with him?

She'd almost seemed excited when he mentioned seeing a murder mystery together. Almost like a real date.

The thought made him smile and spurred him even more to find a theater they could attend this week.

He spent the next half hour searching for the perfect place. Most everything was sold out. Only one he could find was an interactive hippie show, almost an hour northeast. Unfortunately patrons were required to dress up.

He cringed at the thought of wearing bell-bottoms and a bright wide-collared shirt. But the evening could be hilarious.

He called Paige but got her voice mail. He told her what he'd found. "Figured it'd help us get ideas. The show is the day after tomorrow. Thought I'd buy a couple tickets. That night work for you? But I have to warn you that we've got to dress up. Seventies style."

He ended the call and then shifted his attention to finding cheap wood paneling for his renovation. Reclaimed wood would look great, but the price would bust his budget.

Unless…

He remembered the pile of scraps lying beside the partially demolished barn at New Life Furnishings, and his thoughts drifted to Mr. Fischer's place. He had three barns in various stages of decay. That'd provide enough wood to panel the dining-area walls and maybe even two accents in the lobby. Jed could use the metal roofs to detail the stage or for the counters in the lobby. He might even be doing the man a favor, clearing those eyesores off Mr. Fischer's land.

He dialed the man's number.

"Eh-low."

"Howdy, sir. This is Jed Gilbertson, Judith Tappen's grandson."

"Hey, boy. What can I do you for? Everything all right with your nana?"

"She's great. Busy as ever." He explained the reason for his call. "What do you say? Can my buddies and I come tear down your barns for you?"

Mr. Fischer chuckled. "You and your friends can come clean my junk away anytime."

Jed grinned. "I'm much obliged sir, thank you." He grabbed the estimate Drake had given him. The wood from those old barns would save him a pretty penny. Maybe even enough to pay for stained concrete on the floors—with horseshoe prints pressed in.

Things were finally starting to fall into place.

He was about to call his buddies to set up a barn-tearing party when his phone rang. He glanced at the screen. Paige.

"Hey. Thanks for getting back to me."

"You really think I need this? To attend a murder-mystery dinner theater?"

Did he, or was he simply finding an excuse to be with her? He told himself it was the former, but the way he sprang to answer her call indicated otherwise. "It couldn't hurt."

"I don't want to sound rude or anything, but…are you paying? Because…" Her breath reverberated across the line. "I'm broke."

Poor girl. He hated that he'd made her say that out loud. "No problem. This one's on me. Well, on the theater. You know what I mean."

"All right, then. Only—I don't own anything remotely hippy."

Neither did he. "I have an idea. We'll hit the thrift store. My treat."

She laughed. "You always were a big spender."

That sweet, teasing voice got him every time. "I'll pick you up tomorrow morning, at ten?"

"I'll be here."

An image of her wearing a cute little paisley dress with soft curls framing her face triggered a smile.

Then a frown. He'd be wrecked when she left to go back to Chicago.

So he needed to make certain he gave her every reason in the world to stay.

With her hands perched on her hips, Paige studied her mom as she sat behind her computer. She needed a change of scenery—fresh air and to do something fun.

Paige was failing miserably on her get-Mom-out-more campaign. Maybe she needed to take Mira up on her dinner offer one of these nights.

She folded an afghan over the back of the couch. "You sure you're going to be okay? And that you don't mind watching Ava?"

"A quiet afternoon would do me—and this headache I'm fighting—good." Mom rubbed her temples. "Matter of fact, I think I'll join her when she naps. If I'm not doing better by tomorrow, I'll call the doctor."

"If you're not feeling well—"

She waved a hand. "You go on. If I stopped living every time my body chose to revolt, I'd never do anything."

"Maybe the two of you could walk to the park. It's a beautiful day."

The doorbell rang, and she spun around and scrunched the ends of her hair to fluff the curls.

She answered to find Jed on the stoop, dressed in a burnt-orange T-shirt that accentuated his muscular build. She smiled, and the familiar jittery sensation that always hit her whenever his dark eyes latched on to hers swept through her. "Hi."

He tipped his hat at her. "Howdy." He smiled past her. "Mrs. Cordell. Hey there, Ava." His gaze returned to Paige, and warmth was radiating from his eyes. "You ready?"

She nodded, and her mouth suddenly felt dry. "Let me grab my purse." She dashed back inside, paused in her room to inhale a calming breath and check her reflection in the mirror one last time, and then she reemerged.

She snatched Ava up for a firm hug. "You and Grandma have fun."

"Ice cweam?" She reached for the kitchen, opening and closing her hand.

Ava laughed and raised an eyebrow at her mom. "Ice cream, huh? Is that what Grandma feeds you when I'm away?"

Ava bobbed her head with her smile growing.

"That's my job." Mom crossed the room and took Ava from Paige. "Isn't that right, baby girl?" She hugged her close.

Jed laughed. "Sounds about right. Looks like your daughter's in good hands, Paige."

"Apparently." She blew Ava a kiss, waved goodbye to her mom and stepped out.

She closed the door behind her and followed Jed to his truck.

He unlocked it and then reached past her to open her door, and his familiar cologne set her off-kilter.

Her gaze shot to his, and his eyes intensified; his expression became unreadable. But then his lazy grin returned.

It was almost enough to make a girl forget she wasn't interested in romance.

It'd been almost a decade and a half, but her memories from that year still stung. She'd felt so alone. Abandoned. By Jed, her father and even her mom.

It was the same empty-gut feeling she'd had when

she'd arrived home to find her ex-husband standing in their living room with his suitcases packed.

He'd left in much the same way her father had—without much more than a goodbye and zero child support. Once the court had started garnishing her ex's wages, he'd quit his job. She suspected he was working under the table—construction jobs made that easy—but she'd given up chasing him down long ago.

She'd vowed to never become so dependent, emotional or financially, on a man ever again.

But here she sat, falling hard for Jed Gilbertson.

He slid in beside her, making the truck's cab feel entirely too cozy.

He turned on the radio, tuned to the country station and then lowered the sound a notch. "Ever been to The Feather's Bureau?"

"Been a while, but yeah. I went a few times back in high school. Matter of fact, that was where I bought my outfit for the sock hop."

"You went to that?"

"Yeah." And had hated every minute of it. She'd spent the entire night sitting in the back corner with two of her equally shy and awkward friends. The only guy who'd asked her to dance had been Eli Wadlow, a short, buck-toothed kid who talked nonstop about *Pokémon* cards and video games. "Did you?"

He shook his head. "I was too busy pickling my brains at the next party." He turned onto Main Street. "I wasn't the sharpest tool in the shed back then."

He expressed a lot of regret for his past, making it impossible for her to think of him as that dumb jock who'd left her for the popular crowd. In fact, he was demolishing all of her reasons for maintaining her emotional distance, one interaction at a time.

But the most important question still remained: Could she trust him with her—and Ava's—heart?

Thirty minutes later, she headed toward a bright pink dressing room loaded down with polyester clothes in an assortment of colors.

"Wait. Try these, too." His eyes danced as he held up a pair of checkered bell-bottoms. "They'll go great with this." He tossed her a wide beaded headband with rainbow fringe.

"Only if you try that disco ensemble."

His brows shot up, and he stared at the mannequin she pointed to. But then the skin around his eyes crinkled. "Just my style."

By the time they finished, he was carrying a large plastic bag filled with clothes bright enough to be reflective, and Paige's sides ached from laughing.

"You hungry?"

She hesitated. Her heart still hadn't recovered from their lunch after their museum trip. Sitting across a table from him a second time sounded much too intimate. Especially after their little shopping experience. She hadn't had that much fun in some time.

Never could she have imagined Jed Gilbertson swapping his jeans and boots for polyester bell-bottoms. She worked to suppress a giggle.

"What's so funny?"

Taking the hand he offered, she climbed into his truck. "Just thinking what a girl could do with thrift-store-shopping photos." She held up her phone and wiggled it.

His eyes widened. "You wouldn't." He reached for it, and his chest pressed against her shoulder; his face was suddenly very close to hers.

She inhaled sharply; her pulse was accelerating as his gaze held hers.

He stepped back. "On second thought, I should probably get back to the theater."

She straightened and nodded. "I should get home, too."

She was falling in love with Jed all over again, only things were much more complicated this time.

If Paige was going to bring another man into her and Ava's life, she wanted to be certain the man would stay.

Forever.

The next evening, Paige realized she had never worn bright pink before, and the fringe dangling from her headband made her feel ridiculous.

"You look beautiful, sweetie. Don't you agree, Ava?" Mom bopped Ava on the head with her stuffed animal. "Jed Gilbertson is such a nice young man. I'm glad the two of you are spending time together again."

Paige frowned. "Our interaction is purely professional."

"Yes, of course, dear." But her wry smile said otherwise.

Paige sighed as she headed to her bedroom to grab her pocket notebook. Regardless of what her jittery nerves indicated, she was going to this dinner purely for business purposes.

The doorbell rang, and she paused to wipe her sweaty palms on her dress. With a deep breath, she answered.

The image of Jed in a shimmery black, flared-leg '70s disco outfit made her laugh. "I'm sorry. I just— Hi."

His face colored. "Hey." His hand rose toward his head, as if reaching for his hat, which obviously wasn't there, before plunging into his pocket. He glanced past her. "Ma'am."

"Jed." Mom appeared at Paige's side. "Good to see you." She gave Paige a hug. "You two have fun."

The lilt in her voice caused Paige's face to flame. "I'm sure tonight's entertainment will prove very helpful." She crossed the room to hug and kiss Ava, who sat on the floor, surrounded by stuffed animals, and then returned. "Ready?"

Jed smiled. "I was born ready."

On the drive to the theater, they talked about murder mysteries in general and how many he'd attended after buying into his grandparents' business.

"Before then, the only dinner theater I'd ever been to had been Grandma and Grandpa's. I wanted to see how other folks ran things."

"Makes sense."

He shared what he knew about the '70s production, which wasn't much, and she talked about the one time, other than tonight, she'd worn feathers and fringe.

She shook her head. "I don't know why I ever went to that stupid dance. I spent most of the night consoling sobbing friends in the bathroom."

"I bet you were beautiful."

Her gaze met his, and her face turned warm.

Chapter Fifteen

Paige checked her hair in the visor mirror as Jed turned into a parking area in front of a blue house with pink trim and a yellow door. Half a dozen other cars filled the lot with couples stepping from them dressed like *The Brady Bunch* cast members.

A woman with a beehive hairdo and gigantic hoop earrings passed in front of them.

Jed chuckled and cut the engine. "Guess we'll fit right in tonight, huh?"

"Seems like it, although at least we're dressed for the correct era. I think."

Inside the lobby, bright murals covered the walls. Beading draped along the cashier counter, above the windows, and formed a doorway to what likely led to the main dining area. Music she recognized from the '70s poured from hidden speakers.

Jed handed their tickets to a tall man wearing a long blond wig and scraggly beard.

"Table twelve."

Jed nodded and guided Paige into a low-ceilinged room filled with tables covered in tie-dyed linens. "Think we're over there." He pointed to the center of the room, where two other couples sat, and then led her that way. He pulled out the chair for her.

The woman to Paige's right loved to talk. She thought Paige and Jed were "simply adorable." She followed this with a myriad questions about everything from where Paige and Jed had met to how long they'd been dating.

"We're not." Paige fumbled for her glass. "We're just friends." Attempting to avoid further conversation, she watched the couples seated at the other tables.

By the first intermission, however, frequent bouts of laughter had set her at ease. The show was hilarious.

Could she make her script this funny?

She pulled her notebook from her purse. "I'm pretty sure they have cast members placed, incognito, at different tables."

"Like Ms. Chatty, you mean?" Jed tipped his head toward where the woman with the gazillion questions had been sitting before she and her husband had migrated to the hall.

"Hmm." Paige tapped her pencil against her chin. "Know what? I bet you're right."

"You think we should do that?"

"Could be interesting, though it'd probably increase the cast size."

"This seat taken?"

She turned to see a large man dressed in plaid sitting beside her. "Actually, yes, but I think they've gone to the bathroom."

"Their loss. They should learn not to leave such a beautiful woman unattended." He grabbed her hand and leaned forward. "Is he your boyfriend, this man that left you?"

Laughing, she exchanged glances with Jed, who was also chuckling.

"Ah!" The man jerked back with a frown. He crossed his arms and looked from her to Jed, then back to her again. "I see how it is." He stood, dragged his chair to Paige's other side and then attempted to shove it between them. "You and he," he wagged a finger. "No, no, no, no." He glowered at Jed. "What are your intentions toward this lovely woman?"

Jed blinked. "I…uh…excuse me?"

Paige squirmed, feeling as if the entire theater were watching her. They probably were.

"Your intentions." The man jutted his chin. "Declare them now or release her." He grabbed her hand again and kissed the back of it. "Leave this loser and come away with me. He doesn't treat you as you deserve. See? He refuses to proclaim his love in the most romantic of settings. But not I. I am not afraid to tell the entire world about my love for you."

He sprang to his feet with his chair falling to the ground behind him, and held a hand to his heart. "My sweet little flower with such fiery locks, like the very flames of the sun, I love you. Here and now, I say it, for all to hear. I. Love. You."

She slid farther down into her chair as snickers rose all around her. She cast a furtive glance in Jed's direction to find him fixated on his water glass. But then he looked her way, and his eyes held hers. Her breath caught, and she stared at her hands, which were twined tightly in her lap.

"Ricardo, are you harassing the guests again?" Someone approached from behind, and she turned to see a tall blonde woman glaring at Ricardo, as she'd called him with her arms crossed. "Why haven't they fired you already?"

"On account of my beautiful singing voice. Shall I

sing for you now?" He sidled up to her, batting his eyes. "I know how you love to be serenaded, my sweet bouquet of daisies."

The two continued their banter as the guests returned to their seats, and soon the drama was underway again. But the look Jed had given her continued to play on her mind.

On the way home, they once again fell into casual chatter, though it felt stiff. Awkward.

But as they neared Paige's mom's house, Jed grew quiet, serious. As though he were thinking hard about something.

"I have no doubt your Wild West theater is going to be a huge hit," she said.

He pulled up to the curb and then shifted into Park. "Thanks. I really appreciate your help."

"No problem." She tucked a lock of hair behind her ear. "I had a great time tonight. Believe it or not, the drama sparked my muse."

"I'm glad." He rotated toward her. "Listen, Paige, I…" He cleared his throat. "I'm really glad you came tonight."

His deep brown eyes pulled her in.

He leaned closer.

She raised her face to his, feeling her pulse spiking as memories of their most tender moments resurfaced. What would it feel like to be in his strong arms once again?

Then, suddenly, light flashed in her peripheral vision. She jerked back and looked out her window. Lovely. Mom had turned all the lights on and, based on her shadow in the living room window, was watching them.

Making Paige feel like an awkward teenager. Thirty-one years old, living at home with her mom spying on her first date with the grown-up Jed Gilbertson.

Except this wasn't a date.

Was it?

And if it was, what did that mean?

She grabbed her purse from the floorboard. "I better go. I'll see you." She shoved her door open and dashed out.

She was moving back to Chicago soon. Falling in love with him now wasn't a good idea.

The next morning, Jed stopped by New Life Furnishings to check on the status of his order and then headed to his grandmother's.

Nearing the Literary Sweet Spot, an independently owned bakery and bookstore on the end of Main Street, he slowed. Paige sat outside under a tabletop canopy, hunched over an opened notebook. Other materials—books or brochures of some type and a yellow legal pad—were spread out in front of her.

She was probably working on the script. How far had she gotten? Maybe he could help her. He'd enjoyed their brainstorming session much more than he'd anticipated.

And after their outing to the dinner theater, he'd been wondering: Had she felt the same feelings he had? She'd loved him once. Could she do so again? Or had her feelings been nothing more than an immature crush back in high school, one she'd since outgrown?

All these what-ifs were knotting him up inside. He parked along the curb, stepped out of his truck and stood, watching her. She was too engrossed in her work to notice him. After adjusting his Stetson, he hooked a thumb under his belt and ambled over.

He paused a few paces away.

What if he bared his heart and she didn't feel the same? Would things get awkward? She'd still have to finish the script. She'd signed a contract, but their interactions could turn tense. And there was nothing stopping her from leaving town, heading straight for Chicago, once she fulfilled her commitment.

Then again, she planned on doing that anyway, didn't she?

He stepped closer. "Howdy."

She startled and then smiled. "Hey. What're you up to?"

He sat across from her and surveyed the magazines spread out in front of her. A picture of a woman in a black shorts suit with white stripes. Another of a lady in orange heels and silver pants that poufed out from the waist to the knees.

"What's all this?" he asked.

"Back issues of fashion magazines."

"You working on more article queries?"

"Not exactly. I'm... There's a writing conference coming up, and..." Her gaze dropped and then bounced back to his. "I'm hoping to land a job with another magazine."

"Working remotely?"

She shrugged and looked away, almost as if she couldn't look him in the eye. "Those are hard to find."

Meaning she'd likely have to move.

He suddenly realized he wouldn't let her go that easily. Somehow, someway, he'd convince her to stay in Sage Creek. For good.

He scooted his chair closer. "I don't want you to leave, Paige."

"Don't worry—I'll honor my commitment."

"That's not what I mean."

"I'm applying to a lot of places, but there's no guarantee anyone will hire me on."

"If they do? You'll have to move to their offices, wherever that is."

She looked at him for a long moment with her eyes searching his. But then she looked back at the magazines spread out before her.

"I wish I could go back, do things differently. I wish I would've made you listen to me regarding that whole Christy mess. I would've fought for you and kept fighting for you."

Her eyes locked on his, as if trying to read his thoughts. Or maybe deciding whether or not to believe him. But then she shook her head. "That was a long time ago, Jed."

"But you're here now."

"My life has been in flux. In chaos. I'm still trying to get my feet under me."

"So lean on me. I'm not going anywhere."

What would it take for her to believe that?

The look in her eyes said she wanted to. "I need time, Jed."

Chapter Sixteen

Mira's driveway was full when Paige and Mom arrived, so Paige parked along the curb.

"This is it." She eyed the beautiful brick single-story home in front of her. A picture of success with its three-car garage, tall white columns and covered porch. Even her flower bed with its yellow, red and lavender tulips, looked cheery and pristine without a dandelion in sight.

Mom clutched her purse in her lap. "Kinda strange we're invited to a family birthday party. Are you sure they want us here?"

"Of course." Not really, but Mom needed to interact with people, and Paige needed time with her friend. They hadn't been able to connect lately. "Now, come on before we melt." With the engine turned off, the temperature in her car had already begun to climb. "You'll have fun." She flashed a grin, cast a glance at her sleeping little one in the back and opened her door.

"Promise?"

"I can promise there'll be cake." She moved to the back seat to get Ava. "Can you grab the gift bag?"

"Sure." Mom climbed out and then waited in the drive-way for Paige to unbuckle her groggy-eyed little one.

"You ready to play with some kids, sweet girl?" She brushed a kiss against her warm cheek.

Ava rubbed her eyes with fisted hands, looking like the little darling she was. Paige gave her a squeeze, breathing in the sweet scent of her strawberry shampoo.

She and her mom merged onto the walkway and continued to a tall mahogany door. Paige rang the bell and then waited while Mom shifted from foot to foot beside her.

Mira answered wearing an adorable mint-green dress accessorized with a corded leather belt. "Hey. Thanks for coming." She pulled Paige into a hug and then did the same to Mom. "It's so good to see you again, Mrs. Cordell. Oh!" She held a hand to her mouth. "Look at your little one! Hey, sweetie, how are you?" She ran a hand over Ava's head.

Ava buried her face in Paige's shoulder.

"It's been so wonderful having them home." Mom tugged on one of Ava's curls.

"I bet." Mira led the way past a formal living room with cathedral ceilings, and through a tiled kitchen with food covering every surface area.

In the spacious backyard, adults gathered in groups of threes and fours while giggling children ran, skipped and bounced across the lawn. To the far right, a couple of teen boys tossed a Frisbee between them.

"You remember my parents?" Mira looped an arm through Mom's and crossed to where an older couple sat with a handful of others.

"I'm not sure I do." Mom glanced at Paige with a creased brow, looking as though she were about to be thrust into a pack of Black Friday shoppers.

Ava toddled toward an empty sandbox a few feet away.

Paige shifted so she could keep one eye on her while remaining engaged with Mira and her parents.

The conversation felt stilted at first. They asked her about Chicago and how she was enjoying her time in Sage Creek.

They asked her mother what she did for a living.

"I'm a tier-three security-support manager for Phone-Tel Communications," she replied.

"Interesting. Are they based in Texas?" Mira's father asked.

She nodded. "Though we service Fortune 500 companies nationally, our headquarters are in Houston. I telecommute from home."

"How nice."

Mom took a soda Mira offered. "It's so convenient. And with all my health concerns—I've been battling numerous issues for some time…" She rubbed a hand up her arm. "I don't know what I'd do otherwise."

Paige grinned at her friend's parents, who sat side by side with the husband's hand resting on his wife's knee, looking goo-goo-eyed in love. "Mira said the two of you met at an outdoor concert?"

Mira's mom smiled at her husband. "That we did, back when we were both in college. But I was there by accident."

Paige raised an eyebrow. "How's that?"

"My friend dragged me along, but it really wasn't my thing. The music was so loud, and a genre I had no interest in. So I found a quiet place to sit in the shade of a flowering dogwood tree. That's when Donald saw me and decided to make his move."

He laughed. "You were smitten with me from the beginning, and you know it."

"Hardly." She turned to Paige and shook her head.

"But he wouldn't leave me alone. Kept pestering me for my number."

"I wore her down eventually." He winked.

She patted his hand. "That you did, but my parents weren't so quick to join the Donald fan club."

He let out a low whistle. "I'll say. First time I came to pick her up, her father met me with his rifle. Cocked it, then asked me what business I thought I had with his little girl."

"But Donald refused to give up." She twined her fingers with his. "He eventually won my dad over."

Paige smiled. "I love stories like that—where two people fall in love and hold tightly to each other, despite the obstacles."

"Oh, it wasn't like that," Mira's mom said. "I told Donald to go away. Thought we had too much stacked against us."

He wrapped an arm around his wife's shoulder and tugged her closer. "Good thing I didn't listen to her—otherwise she would've missed out on the best thing that ever happened to her."

She gave him a playful swat. "Took a stubborn man like Donald to teach me love's worth the risk. Truth is I used my parents as an excuse, but I was scared. Scared of what would happen if I let myself fall too deep and things didn't work out."

Paige's mind flashed to Jed, and her stomach flip-flopped.

Was her fear of getting hurt again keeping her from experiencing the love she'd always hoped for?

The rest of the afternoon, though she did her best to stay engaged in the various conversations, her mind kept drifting back to that question.

She had a lot to think through, but one thing was

certain. She wouldn't gain any clarity from avoiding Jed—or her feelings for him.

Jed removed his Stetson and swiped a rag across his sweaty forehead. The late-morning air felt sticky and thicker than a midsummer storm cloud. At least they hadn't disrupted any copperheads during their demolition.

Mr. Fischer's barns had been better off than Jed had suspected. Other than some jagged fragments scattered across the tall grass, most of the wood was usable. Seemed they'd salvaged enough to panel the theater's walls and floor the lobby. Maybe even with some left over for accents.

Drake pulled off his gloves and grabbed a water bottle from a nearby cooler. "Want one?"

Jed nodded, and his buddy tossed one his way, and then threw others to the rest of their crew.

He took a long drink of water, then removed his hat and poured the rest over his head. "Appreciate you fellas helping me clear all this out." He grabbed himself a second bottle.

"Wait a minute." Drake sauntered over to Jed. "You're paying us, right? Figured I'd tag this on to my remodel invoice."

"Oh, I'll pay you all right." Jed gave him a playful shove. "With a five-buck knuckle sandwich."

Drake laughed, picked up a piece of straw by his boots and stuck it in his mouth. "What about the rest of this?" He motioned toward the wood splinters spread out across the field. "Want us to stick around to clean all this up?"

"The smaller pieces will decompose, but I figure we best do something with the rest of it. What do you think about lighting a big ol' fire and roasting some dogs on it like we used to?"

Drake and the others, four in all, grinned, and each voiced his enthusiasm for the idea.

"I'll call my wife." Seth, a buddy from way back, leaned against the side of his truck and pulled his phone from his shirt pocket. "See what she's got going on."

"Tell her to bring a pot of her baked beans, heavy on the bacon." Drake took a long swig of his water and glanced to another one of their buddies, who was still pulling rusted nails from wood planks. "Hey, Ty, think Shelby will make a jug of her sweet tea?"

Tyler shrugged, carried a plank of wood to his truck and then tossed it in the back. "Probably. Soon's we unload all this, I'll give her a call."

All the talk about calling their women to bring them to the cookout made Jed acutely aware of his single status. That fact hadn't bothered him—until now, when his thoughts kept drifting to Paige. But he didn't want to push too hard and risk scaring her off. He knew she had a lot to process, and that everything probably felt all jumbled in her heart and brain after all she'd gone through during and after her divorce.

But he also didn't want to give her so much space that she would up and take off for Chicago.

He'd lost her once, but God had brought her back to Sage Creek. That had to mean something, right?

With all of their trucks loaded, Jed and his buddies drove to his dinner theater. He entered to find the place in the latter stages of demolition.

Forty minutes later, he and the guys had all but one truck unloaded, and Jed was covered in grime, sawdust and sweat. He could sure use some of that sweet tea Tyler's girlfriend made. And a big slab of venison, slowly roasted over open flames.

He deposited his handful of boards along the wall and then turned for more. Then he stopped. Paige stood in front of him, dressed in jean shorts and a ruffled blouse with a scoop neckline.

"Hey." She fiddled with her bracelet. "Um… Are you busy?"

He pulled the hand towel he'd been carting around from his back pocket and mopped the sweat from his face. He could feel his buddies eyeing him, probably wondering what was up with Paige and him talking again.

"Let's go to my office." He led the way, ignoring the soft chuckle from one of his buddies behind him.

When they reached his office, he considered keeping the door open to stop folks from flapping their jaws more than they already would be. But with all of the banging, hammering and sawing Drake's crew was doing, the place was too loud for decent conversation. And Paige's pinched expression told him whatever she wanted to say would be awkward enough.

"Have a seat." He motioned to the chair in front of his desk and then sat across from her. "Everything all right?"

She nodded and then took a deep breath. "I enjoyed going out with you the other night. To the dinner theater."

So that was what this was about.

"It reminded me of old times." Her crystal-blue eyes studied his with her delicate brow furrowed. But then her features relaxed into the most genuine smile he'd seen from her in some time. "Before…you know."

He nodded. "Want to talk about it?"

"I think we should."

"You have to know I never cheated on you."

"But you didn't really stick around, either. I needed you, Jed. It felt like my life was falling apart."

"I know." He released a breath. "And I'm sorry." Something told him this was about much more than him. It'd all gotten jumbled together in her mind—her dad bailing, their family struggling financially, her mom withdrawing emotionally. "I didn't leave you, Paige. You pulled away from me."

"What are you talking about?"

"You changed. You were so…angry. All the time." He winced. That sounded bad. "Like you wanted nothing to do with me."

"That didn't seem to bother you much. You were too busy chasing cheerleaders to notice."

"That's not true. Things were hard for me, too. My dad alternated from giving me the cold shoulder to telling me how I was never going to succeed in life. On account of I didn't want to be a lawyer like him. My mom was nagging me all the time to make a college decision—a life decision. The pressure was too much, you know?"

Her eyes searched his, and the edge within them softened some.

He released a breath. "I felt like I was failing everyone, especially you. I didn't know how to handle it, so I didn't. I just quit thinking about it all—about everything. I started hanging out at parties. But I didn't leave you. I couldn't have. You'd already left."

"I was upset and totally freaked out. You knew that."

"I should've held tight to you. We should've held tight to each other."

Silence stretched between them, but then she inhaled and smiled. "Seems to me you never quite responded to Ricardo's challenge."

"Ricardo…?" He grinned. "I see how that could be

a problem." He rose and rounded his desk, fighting the urge to pull her close and kiss her. "So, tell me, Paige Cordell, are you saying—?"

"Why do you have to put everything into a box?" An old phrase he used often in high school, whenever she tried to overthink things.

He chuckled. "Using my words against me, I see."

"Something like that. So...now what?"

"Guess maybe we'll figure that out as we go?" As much as he wanted to lasso her for good, he knew he needed to take things slowly. To prove he planned to stand beside her and Ava for good.

"The fellas and I are throwing a cookout tonight. Want to come?"

She didn't respond right away, then took a deep breath and nodded. "Sure. Yeah, I'll go."

That was a start.

Paige stepped back from the billowing fire and grabbed a soda from the cooler near Jed's truck. She tried to tell herself it was the thick smoke swirling toward her that caused her eyes and nose to sting, but it was more than that.

She felt as though she'd regressed to that shy, awkward teenager who always felt like the outsider. This was Jed's world—boots, cowboy hats and cookouts.

She fit much better in Chicago. There, people accepted her for who she was.

No. They left her alone. Allowed her to believe her self-imposed isolation was normal.

And the busyness and traffic and constant noise allowed her to distract herself from the loneliness invading her heart.

A loneliness she hadn't felt lately. Not since she and Jed had been hanging out again.

She sat at the base of an old, gnarled oak tree. With her back pressed against the rough trunk, she hugged her legs to her chest and rested her chin on her knees. She watched as Jed's buddies laughed and carried on.

Was there room in their world for her?

Did she truly belong back in Sage Creek?

Jed stepped back from the fire and looked around. He strolled over. "You all right?"

"Just tired, I guess."

He lowered to the ground beside her; his shoulder felt warm against hers. "You sure? Because seems to me you clammed up the minute Tyler's girlfriend arrived. She didn't give you any trouble, did she?"

Paige plucked a blade of grass. "No. It's just…" She sighed. "Never mind."

"Don't do this, Paige."

"Do what?"

"Hide behind that protective shell of yours. If we're going to give this a go between us, we've got to do things differently. We owe ourselves that much."

"I guess." How would she know what it took to make a relationship work? She hadn't exactly had the best role models in her parents. Nor had she done any better than they had with her own marriage.

"So, tell me—" he nudged her shoulder with his "—what's gotten you so quiet?"

She gazed toward the fire, wishing she could verbalize all of her emotions. Wishing she understood her feelings herself. "Your friends don't like me."

"They hardly know you."

"They know what they remember."

"And what's that?"

She shrugged.

He cupped her chin in his callused hand and turned her face toward him. "Like I said, they don't know you. Because you haven't given them a chance. Instead, you're seeing rejection that isn't there. Besides, who cares what they think? I sure don't."

Her breath caught as he leaned closer. His lips brushed against hers, causing her insides to melt.

Someone whooped, and she jolted backward, whacking her head on the tree behind her. Snickers erupted.

Jed shook his head. "What is this, junior high?"

Paige smiled. "Apparently."

Except, for once she no longer felt like the awkward, frizzy-haired middle schooler. Maybe Sage Creek wasn't so terrible after all.

Suddenly she was rethinking her plans to return to Chicago. She knew she couldn't live in her mother's guest room forever, not to mention she was a journalist, not a scriptwriter. Besides, for all she knew, Jed's theater could go bust before summer's end. By then she could be employed with a prestigious, well-paying magazine, if everything went well at the writers' conference.

But could she give up her dreams of making it in the magazine world for Jed?

Could she give up Jed for the life she'd left in Chicago?

Chapter Seventeen

Jed stomped muck from his boots and then entered into his parents' mudroom, where he took them off entirely.

Dad's voice drifted from the kitchen. He must've cut his business trip short, probably because of the basement flooding. And likely he wasn't in the best of moods.

Jed strode down the hall and around the corner. He touched the brim of his hat and gave a quick dip of his head. "Pop."

"Son. Thanks for coming out. For keeping an eye on things while I was gone."

Jed nodded and faced his mother. "I talked to my contractor buddy about your wood floors. He said he'll call next week to schedule a time to come give you an estimate." The basement flooding had caused the wood floors in the half bath to buckle.

"He'll work with the insurance company?" Mom set her towel on the counter and crossed her arms.

He nodded. "Shouldn't be a problem."

"Thanks for your help." Dad clamped a hand on Jed's shoulder. "Now that that's taken care of—" he glanced around "—when's supper?"

Mom's eyes lit. "Let's go out to eat."

He sighed. "Jillian, I just walked in the door not ten minutes ago."

"Come on. When's the last time Jed had a night off? Besides, I don't have anything thawed."

Dad frowned. "You're not going to let up, are you?"

Mom grinned. "Just give me a minute to freshen up."

Twenty minutes later, they pulled into Wilma's parking lot, where his sister and brother-in-law would be meeting them. Hopefully the conversation would remain light.

Jed glanced at the time on his phone. How was Paige doing? She was probably packing for that writing conference she was going to.

The one she hoped would somehow get her back to Chicago.

Dare he hope she'd change her mind? Stay in Sage Creek?

He'd find out soon enough.

Paige cast her mom a sideways glance and placed the last clean towel, now folded, into the hamper. "Are you sure you don't want to come?"

"You go. Mira's your friend. I'd feel silly intruding."

"She wouldn't bat an eye—promise. I really think you'll feel better if you get out for a bit." As far as she knew, Mom hadn't left the house in two days. Not even to visit Mrs. Tappen. Would she be okay while Paige was away at the writing conference? She was scheduled to fly out first thing in the morning. Maybe she should cancel her trip.

But she didn't want to blow her chance at meeting some of the top magazine publishers in the nation. And what about Jed? Could she really leave him, move to

Chicago or Minneapolis, or wherever else her career demanded?

Mom wrapped both hands around her steaming mug of tea and shook her head. "What I need is a good, long nap. To rest these aching bones."

Paige frowned. Depression could make someone hurt, right? Wasn't that what the commercials said? "You can rest at Wilma's, and I'll bring you back right after."

"Quit worrying, sweetie. And tell Mira hello for me." She smiled. "It's so nice to see you reconnecting with your old friends." Mom's knowing smile implied she meant friends other than just Mira. As if she knew how Paige's heart skipped whenever her thoughts shifted to Jed—which was constantly.

But as much as she cared for him, they still had so much to figure out. They came from completely different worlds. His parents had always hated her. Though his mom never came right out and said so, her curt tone and pinched expression had made it clear that she thought Paige was beneath him.

She was trying to be smart about all of this, but each day, with every conversation, Jed was dismantling all of her logical reasons for why they wouldn't make it.

Though the past still stung, she'd forgiven him. Like he'd said, they'd both been dealing with issues at home, and Paige had withdrawn, from him and everyone else. She'd just been so sad. Scared. Confused.

She'd pulled away from him much in the same way Mom had pulled away from her.

How much of the ache she felt came from her breakup with Jed, and how much was from the rejection she felt from her father?

There was no sense in brooding over the past. Tonight

she planned to have fun with her friend and eat ginormous quantities of junk food.

And try not to stress about her and Jed's burgeoning relationship. And the writing conference. And her decision whether or not to return to Chicago.

Less than twenty minutes later, she sat in a restaurant across from her childhood best friend with a massive platter of nachos between them.

She scooped guacamole onto a chip. "Honestly, I feel like an idiot for going."

"Why?" Mira sipped her sweet tea.

"Oh, I don't know. Maybe the fact that I'm chasing after a dream that, if my recent layoff is any indication, I'm incapable of."

Mira rolled her eyes. "Way to be overdramatic, Paige."

"All right, so maybe I'm not entirely inept—"

"Far from it."

"But writing is a competitive field. Who's to say I'm not wasting my time and money going to this thing?"

"Is this what you really want?"

If Mira had asked her that question a couple of weeks ago, Paige would've responded with a resounding yes. Now she wasn't sure.

"I need to use the restroom." She set her napkin on the table and stood.

Mira took a sip of water. "We can finish this conversation when you get back."

Paige smiled and made her way toward the back of the restaurant.

Halfway there, her gaze swept across a table of five, and she halted. Her heart gave a leap. "Jed." She smiled.

His eyebrows shot up. "Howdy." He looked first to his mom, then to his dad. "Uh… You remember my… uh…friend Paige."

Friend? It wasn't just the word, but the way he said it that made her tense. Was he ashamed of her?

"Of course. Marilyn Cordell's daughter." His mom's features tightened, and then she slid a glance toward her husband. "Jed offered her a job at his theater."

"Oh?" Mr. Gilbertson scooped fajita meat onto a tortilla. "That's nice."

His wife nodded. "You may have heard she lost her job in Chicago."

Paige's mouth dropped open, and her throat suddenly felt tight and scratchy.

"Mom." Jed's voice was low.

Mrs. Cordell dipped a fry into her ketchup. "Which reminds me, I need to pick up a few more auction items for the charity ball. Jed, would you mind asking your buddy Michael if he'll donate some of his wonderful handcrafted items? It's for such a great cause."

Paige's face grew hot. She and her mom reminded Mrs. Gilbertson of a charity function?

A cell phone trilled, and Mrs. Gilbertson glanced at her screen. "Excuse me. I need to take this." She pushed away from the table. "Aileen, hello…"

Paige stepped back to allow her by and then offered a stiff smile first to Jed's mother, and then to him. "Enjoy your meal."

"I'll call you."

Ignoring Jed, she walked to the bathroom and locked herself in the stall to give herself a moment to calm down. To throw off the sting of rejection she always seemed to feel whenever Mrs. Cordell was around.

But she refused to allow that woman to spoil her night. She'd enjoy her time with Mira, get a good night's sleep and have an amazing time at the writer's conference tomorrow. Where people would evaluate her based on her skill set, not her past or where she came from.

With a deep breath, she fluffed her hair and pushed open the bathroom door.

Mrs. Cordell's voice, drifting from the hall, stopped her. "The Cordell girl. Oh, I know. It's so sad. Mental illness is hereditary, you know."

Old insecurities, the ones that had plagued her throughout high school, came rushing back.

Paige shook them off, squared her shoulders and stepped out into the hall.

Mrs. Cordell's eyes widened when they landed on Paige.

She jetted her chin. "Ma'am."

No one could make Paige feel like trash unless she let them.

But why put herself in that position in the first place? Clearly, Mrs. Cordell felt Jed was too good for her. What would family reunions and Christmas dinners be like?

How would Mrs. Cordell treat her sweet Ava?

It was one thing to endure personal rejection; it was another matter entirely to willingly expose her daughter to it.

Once dinner was over, Jed excused himself and hurried to his truck to call Paige. She'd clearly been upset when she'd left their table, and understandably so. His mother had no right to make Paige feel so small. And knowing her with all of her five-year plans and thought processes, she was probably fretting over what she might have to endure should she and Jed merge their lives together.

He just needed to convince her that it wouldn't be an issue.

Which meant he needed to have a firm and clear conversation with his mom.

But first he wanted to talk to Paige.

Unfortunately he got her voice mail, so he left a message. "It's me. I'm sorry about tonight. I know you're probably upset. And I understand why. But I'll deal with my mom." He released a heavy breath. "Don't let her ugliness get between us. Please."

Jed ended the call and prayed it wasn't too late.

Paige trudged up the Chicago O'Hare Jetway, carrying her computer bag on one shoulder and her carry-on on the other. As she neared an airport coffee shop, the rich scent of fresh roast and cinnamon baked goods made her empty stomach rumble. She pulled her phone from her back pocket and checked the time. Just after eight o'clock, which allowed her nearly an hour to buy her caffeine-and-sugar fix, grab a taxi and make it to the conference center.

Was this a mistake? What if she was no good, and that'd been the real reason the magazine had let her go?

Then this whole trip would be a waste of time and money. She felt guilty enough, and even a little irresponsible, considering the state of her bank account, blowing round-trip airfare for a one-day conference that could easily amount to zilch.

But she refused to become her own limiting factor by paralyzing herself with doubts. She had more important ways to keep her brain occupied, like presenting herself well.

Standing in line in front of the bakery counter, she pulled a typed slip of paper from her computer bag and reviewed her bio.

She inhaled a deep breath and mentally rehearsed what she hoped to say to the editors she'd encounter. Hopefully they still had appointment openings. Apparently,

Paige had registered later than most of the other writers. The online form said appointment registrations had been closed, but that attendees might be able to sign up for last-minute openings the day of. In other words, Paige really needed registrants not to show or to change their minds.

If any of them were experiencing the same precon-ference jitters as she was, she stood a reasonably good chance of that.

She practiced her article pitches a few more times in the cab ride to Juliet, then again as she waited outside the cavernous appointment room. All of her ideas felt... bland. Ordinary and overdone. But they were all she had.

"You going in?"

She turned to see a tall bald man standing beside her.

"I...um... Is this where we make appointments to meet with editors?"

He nodded. "Go on in. The tables have signs showing who's where and sheets on them listing available time slots. Mr. Edwards from Ink Splotch won't be here until this afternoon."

"Thanks." She turned back to the room and then froze. Ardell Dannheim was walking toward her, looking at her phone. If Paige moved fast, she could dart away before her former boss saw her.

Or she could hold her head high and act like the pro-fessional she was.

Before she'd made a decision, Ardell glanced up, and her steps slowed. A deep groove formed between her pencil-thin eyebrows. "Ms. Cordell, good to see you."

She swallowed. "You, as well." How could *Chic Fash-ions* magazine send a representative to a conference de-signed to connect editors with writers after having just laid off a quarter of their staff?

"How have you been?"

"Well. Staying busy."

"That's good to hear." She paused. "I heard you moved."

"I am on…an extended vacation of sorts. Helping my mom out in Texas."

"I see." She shifted her briefcase to her other arm. "Who are you meeting with?"

She glanced past her, toward the open appointment room. "I haven't gotten that far yet."

"Come by my table. I'm representing *East Coast Bling*."

Paige blinked. "You left *Chic Fashions*?"

Ardell cracked a wry smile. "Writers weren't the only ones to get the boot."

"Wow. I didn't know, Ardell. I'm sorry to hear that."

"It happens. Poor business planning and financial management hurts everyone." She looked up as a stream of writers dressed in slacks, blouses and blazers hustled past her. "Looks like it's that time. I've got a class to teach. If you want to learn how to turn passé story ideas into editor-grabbing queries, join us."

"I just might do that."

She watched the woman she'd once blamed for her layoff hurry down the hall, suddenly looking…human. And potentially like someone who could help Paige restart her journalism career.

With a burst of hope and renewed confidence, she turned back to the appointment room, which was now practically empty.

Her phone, set on silent, vibrated in her back pocket. She glanced at the screen and sighed. Jed had called again. She wasn't ready to talk to him—about their relationship, his parents, what their future might look like if they were together…

Where Paige would be a year or even a month from now was hard to say.

Could she commit to something permanent with Jed, the man she loved, knowing his parents might forever hate her? If she did, how long would it be before the tension began to tear them apart? How long before she began to resent him, or he her?

And what about her poor, sweet Ava?

She played the voice message.

"Hey. It's Jed. I know today will be busy for you, but can we talk when you get a chance?" He paused. "About the restaurant last night and…my mom?"

She shot him a quick text. Soon. Then she tucked her phone into her back pocket.

Chapter Eighteen

Standing in his office, Jed sifted through the box of costumes Grandma had brought. "These are perfect."

She grinned. "I hoped you'd like them. Of course, if we need to make any last-minute adjustments to fit the cast, I'm sure that won't be a problem."

"We're short on time with the reopening being a week from today."

"I know, but the ladies are prepared to work quickly. That reminds me, did Paige ever get our press release written?"

He nodded. "I sent it out to our media contacts a few days ago."

"Good. That girl's been such a blessing. You better not go scaring her off."

"I'll try not to." If only he could get his mom to say the same.

With Paige's contract officially ending a week from today, there wasn't much to hold her in Sage Creek. Would she stay in Texas for him? Or was she still set on returning to Chicago?

If he didn't find a way to deal with his mother, he worried there was no point.

Grandma shuffled toward the desk, gripped the chair's armrests and lowered herself behind the computer.

The front door chimed. "That must be New Life Furnishings delivering our stuff." He couldn't wait to see the finished products, arranged in the newly redone theater. The place was going to look amazing, and the final script Paige had sent over before leaving for her conference had been fantastic. Hilarious and filled with questions and clues, including false ones.

With steps lightened by a hope he hadn't felt since he had bought into his grandparents' business, he exited the office. He continued down the short hall to the dining/theater area and then halted.

"Paige."

"Hey." She stood a few feet from the archway leading to the lobby, dressed in tan shorts and an aqua blouse. She wore her hair pulled back with tight ringlets framing her sun-kissed face.

"How was your writing conference?"

"Good." She studied him with a furrowed brow, as if she were worried about something.

"Thanks for stopping by." The sad yet resolute look in her eyes suggested he wasn't going to like what she came to say, as if she'd made up her mind already, regardless of how their conversation went.

"Is now a good time?"

"Sure. Let's go to the office."

She nodded and followed him with her sandaled feet making a soft scuffing noise on the carpet. Each hesitant footstep added to the weight settling on his heart. He wasn't ready for her to leave. He wanted her to be happy, sure. He just wished she could be happy here with him.

When he entered his office, Grandma glanced up with her spectacles balanced on the end of her nose. Her gaze shifted to Paige, who was standing beside him, and she sprang to her feet. "Hello, dear! How good to see you." But then her features tightened, and her eyes shifted between the two of them. "Is something wrong?"

Jed swallowed. "Can we have a minute?"

Her deepening frown indicated she felt the same foreboding he did. "Certainly." She crossed the room and reached for Paige's hand. "Let's talk later. I'd love to hear about your trip."

Paige nodded.

"The furniture folks will be here any minute." Jed handed Grandma his receipt, which listed the details of their order. "Think you can direct them where to put everything?"

"I've been running this place since you were in diapers." She tapped the brim of his Stetson. "I'm pretty sure I can tell those men where to put tables and chairs."

He smiled. "Right."

She left, humming an old country tune he vaguely recognized.

"Have a seat." He motioned to the chair in front of his desk, shifted some papers and sat on the corner. "Listen, I know my mom can be..." He didn't want to speak about her disrespectfully, but this was something he absolutely needed to address. "I'll talk to her."

"And say what? Tell her to stop hating me?"

"She doesn't hate you."

"Well, she's not exactly my biggest fan."

"It's not you. She's always been a bit...protective of me."

"It's not healthy. Not for us, not for our marriage—if we were to get married. Not for Ava."

He sighed. "I know. Like I said, I'll talk to her."

"And you think she'll listen? And change?"

"She'll have to."

"Or what?"

"I'll stand by you. You know that." He'd fight for Paige with everything within him, but he couldn't just cut his mom out of his life. Nor could he demand she suddenly embrace Paige.

But he could pray, something he should've done a long time ago.

Later that afternoon, he met his mother at the Literary Sweet Spot. The scent of chocolate, cinnamon and freshly roasted coffee filled the air.

They chose a table tucked in the far corner. The whir of the espresso machine challenged their hearing, but it would also provide his mom a level of privacy he hoped would make their conversation easier.

"Is everything okay?" She wrapped both hands around her steaming mug.

"We need to talk about Paige."

Her face hardened. "I'm listening."

"I love her."

She stared at him, then leaned against her seat back, looked beyond him and took a slow sip of her coffee.

"Mom."

"I heard you."

"What do you have against her?"

"I've told you. When you marry a girl, you marry her family."

"And she'd be marrying into mine. Which is precisely why we need to talk."

His mom took in a sharp breath. "How dare you."

"I love her. She—"

"Has a child."

"She and her daughter, Ava, bring me joy. I lost Paige

once. I won't lose her again. I won't let you drive her from me."

"What are you saying?"

"I'm saying I plan to spend the rest of my life with that woman. Every Christmas, Thanksgiving, Sunday dinners, vacations… To build a life with her."

Her eyes grew moist, and she dropped her gaze.

He placed his hand over hers. "I'd love for you and Dad to be a part of that. For you to get to know her—to see the amazing, creative, fun, contemplative, brilliant woman I've fallen in love with. To get to know that sweet child of hers. But I can't force you. Neither can I let you rob me of the best gift God's given me."

"What are you saying? It's her or me?"

"It doesn't have to be that way." He pushed his chair back and stood. "I love you both. But I refuse to lose her, Mom."

Paige absentmindedly watched Ava stack storage bowls, one inside the other. At this moment, Jed was talking to his mother, and Paige had little hope that conversation was going well. Love wasn't supposed to be this hard. She'd never wanted to come between Jed and his mom.

What if Mrs. Gilbertson didn't budge? What if she became enraged and stormed out, or gave Jed an ultimatum?

Would he still choose Paige?

Would she want him to, if it cost him his relationship with his mom?

"You all right?" Sitting at the table, Mom peered at Paige over her glasses.

"Just antsy."

"Hmm… Me, too. Want to go to Wilma's for a slice of apple pie?"

"Not really." Mira had offered the same thing—followed by buckets of ice cream and sappy chick flicks that would only make Paige cry.

"Well—" Mom stood "—I for one don't want to spend my Saturday doing paperwork." She pulled off her reading glasses and set them on top of a stack of manila files on her desk. "What do you say we get some ice cream?"

"Ice cweam?" Ava looked at her grandma with big, hopeful eyes. Always such a sunshine.

"What is this, sugar day?"

"What are you talking about?"

"Mira suggested I drown my sorrows in carbs, too."

"What sorrows?"

"Oh, you know, the adulting kind, but they'll pass."

"With a sufficient dose of chocolate, I'm sure."

"And a cinnamon-roll latte." Paige gave her daughter a squeeze.

Mom stood and deposited her coffee mug in the sink. "You got any writing you need to finish first?"

"Not really." She'd finished the mystery script, and Jed had said he liked it, it was hilarious, and it would keep his patrons on their toes.

"All right, then. Are we leaving anytime soon?" Mom grabbed her purse off the floor by her chair. "Or are you just going to sit there moping?"

"Sorry." Paige gathered her things and Ava, and then she followed Mom outside into the hot, sticky air.

An engine hummed, drawing closer and then lingering. She straightened and glanced toward the sound. Her heart stuttered. It was Jed and his grandmother.

Mrs. Tappen grinned at her and stepped from the vehicle. "Paige, Marilyn, you've got to see the costumes the gals at Trinity Faith made for the theater reopening." She waved them over, and before Paige could protest, Mom hurried her way. Soon the two were engaged in conversation.

Paige followed. She shot a glance in Jed's direction. His eyes held hers for a moment, as if pleading.

She wished she had an answer for him, or a different answer than she felt she needed to give.

Maybe it'd be best for them both if they ended things now, before things turned ugly between him and his mom.

"Come in." Mrs. Tappen looped an arm through Paige's and urged her toward her house. "I think you'll be pleased."

She glanced at Jed once again to find him watching her, but his face was too shadowed by his Stetson to make out what he might be thinking. Though she could assume.

She'd never been more convinced of his love, nor had she ever been more uncertain of their future.

She suppressed a sigh as a heaviness settled in her chest. The familiar sense of loneliness and abandonment crept in. She knew better than to let her heart get tangled in a romance with Jed Gilbertson. Hadn't she learned her lesson the first time?

When they reached Mrs. Tappen's stoop, she began to rummage through her purse, still talking about the costumes.

"I hope you'll like the colors we chose." She pulled out keys dangling from a neon-green lanyard. "We went with cool colors for the women's dresses—used some images I found online as reference points." She unlocked her door, opened it and then cast a glance over her shoulder. "Can you grab the boxes from the back of your truck, Jed? Including the fabric for the lobby and gift-store display window? I want to show them to Paige and Marilyn. Maybe you ladies could give me some ideas." She opened her arms to take Ava, and Paige handed her over. "I could use help in the creative department."

The scent of fresh bread and a hint of cinnamon wafted toward Paige as she entered, reminding her of the countless afternoons she'd spent at Mrs. Tappen's breakfast bar, eating freshly baked goodies and talking about movies and books. Occasionally their conversations turned more serious, when Paige wanted advice, which usually involved her dad. Inevitably, Jed would show up, and he and Paige would walk to the bookstore for giant cookies.

In the kitchen, Paige sat beside Mom at the breakfast counter while Mrs. Tappen pulled plates from the cupboard. "You ladies up for something sweet?" She grabbed a spatula from a ceramic utensil holder and pulled a tray of cinnamon rolls, freshly baked—if the smell was any indication—toward her.

"You know I can never turn down anything you make," Mom said.

Mrs. Tappen placed a tub of butter on the counter. "What about you, sugar?"

"I…" Paige's gaze zipped to Jed, who entered carrying two cardboard boxes stacked on top of one another. When their eyes met, he hesitated, and her heart skittered.

"Can we talk?" His eyes searched hers. "Later?"

"Sure."

He placed his load on the counter between her and his grandmother.

Mrs. Tappen looked from him to Paige with a furrowed brow and then proceeded to dish rolls onto plates, distributing them and forks to each of them. After serving herself, she rummaged through the first box Jed had brought in while he leaned against the arched entryway.

"This used to be a curtain—can you believe it?" Mrs. Tappen pulled out wine-colored velvet that was bordered with golden tassels. "One of the ladies snagged it at a garage sale for five bucks. Got the fringe on clearance at the craft store."

"Nice." Mom ran her hand across the fabric. "So, where will this go, then?"

"I was figuring on the counter by the cash register, though Jed might have other ideas."

Paige sat with a heavy confused heart as Mrs. Tappen pulled one item after another out of her box. Each time her mother *oohed* and *ahed* and asked questions regarding placement. Paige feigned interest, shooting frequent glances to Jed.

She was anxious yet nervous to hear what he'd have to say. She didn't feel right about him confronting his mom, considering she still wasn't certain she planned to stay in Sage Creek.

Would her decision come more easily if she knew the tension between her and Jed's mom might abate? If she thought they might even get along eventually?

"We better get those back to the theater, don't you think?" Jed asked.

Mrs. Tappen glanced at the microwave clock behind her. "Oh, my. Yes, I suppose we should."

Ten minutes later, with items folded and returned to their box, Paige and Mom followed Jed and Mrs. Tappen out. He loaded the costumes in his truck while the ladies chatted. Feeling like a swatch of polyester in a sequined gown, Paige walked to her mother's car to wait and leaned against the back bumper.

Hadn't she known this would happen? That falling in love with Jed again would only lead to pain?

Jed approached a moment later.

A breeze stirred a lock of hair against her cheek. She tucked it behind her ear. "How'd your talk go?"

He blew out a puff of air and rubbed the back of his neck. "About how I'd expected."

"What does that mean?"

"Give her time."

In other words, nothing had changed.

"Trust me on this, Paige. I won't let her get between us."

If only it was really that easy.

Apparently done with her conversation with Mrs. Tappen, Mom ambled over, holding Ava in her arms. She glanced at Jed. "We're about to get ice cream. Care to join us?"

He looked to Paige, as if seeking her invite. When she didn't respond, he said, "I should probably head back to the theater. My crew will be showing up for rehearsals soon." He grabbed Paige's hand. "But I'd like to see you. Tomorrow?"

She wanted to say yes, to spend every moment possible with him. But considering all that lay in flux, it'd be wiser to distance herself. "I need time to process some things."

Crease lines formed above his brow. He nodded, gave her hand a squeeze and then dropped it.

Paige unlocked the car and climbed in. Hot air clogged her lungs, and the vinyl seat cushions burned the back of her legs.

After placing Ava in her car seat, Mom slid behind the steering wheel and took the keys. She cranked the engine, sending a gust of sun-heated air through the vents.

She watched Jed and Mrs. Tappen climb into his truck, and then she looked at Paige. "What was that about?"

"What do you mean?" Tears stung her eyes. Less than a month home, and her heart felt broken again.

"You and Jed were acting awful strange." Mom backed out of her drive. "Like you both just lost your best friends. You didn't break up, did you?"

Paige fastened her seat belt and turned on the radio. "It's complicated, Mom."

"Sweetie, don't let one disagreement get in the way of a good thing."

"That's not it."

"Well, whatever it is, it seems to me, when you love someone, you got to hold on to them." She turned onto Dodger Street. "Sometimes I wonder if someone had told your father that, if we'd still be together now. Guess he thought leaving was just easier."

Paige's heart squeezed painfully. Wasn't that exactly how she'd been acting toward Jed?

She had no say over her father's behavior, but she had full control over hers. She didn't have to follow in his footsteps.

Chapter Nineteen

On Sunday afternoon, Jed took Grandma to Wilma's Kitchen for lunch so she could satisfy her fried catfish cravings.

She moved her napkin aside and then repositioned her silverware on it. "I sure wish Paige and her mama could've joined us."

He focused on his menu, even though he knew every item Wilma served by heart.

She moved her place setting aside and leaned forward, resting her arms on the table. "What's going on with you two?"

"What do you mean?"

"Don't go all tight-lipped on me, Jed."

He raised his menu a notch and skimmed the page, without seeing any of it. Most likely he'd get the three-cheese sundried-tomato omelet.

"You two been down this road once already," she said. "Time to start doing things different, if you ask me. That girl's worth hanging on to. She's stubborn as all get out, sure. Got a feisty side. But she's got a good heart, and she loves you something fierce."

"That might not be enough."

"Love's always enough. And it always hopes, always trusts and always perseveres."

Her gaze locked on something past his left shoulder, and her eyes rounded.

"What is it?" He followed her line of vision to the mounted television set, to see police lead his father away in handcuffs. The caption read Owner of Gilbertson Law Firm Arrested for Fraud. Jed blinked. This couldn't be real.

He continued watching as an officer guided his father into the back of a police car.

This had to be a mistake. False accusations made by a disgruntled client. He grabbed his phone off the table and saw Grandma doing the same thing. He tried his dad, but got his voice mail.

Grandma held a hand to her throat. "This is your mother. I... Call me."

On Monday morning, Paige took Ava for a walk around Mirror Lake, to catch a few quiet moments to think. As she pushed Ava's stroller down the paved walkway, birds chirped, and an uncharacteristically cool breeze swept over them. Mom had been bugging her relentlessly about Jed, pestering her to not let outside obstacles stand in the way of their relationship.

But it wasn't that easy. If she'd learned anything from her divorce, it was that marriage was hard. Those challenges one felt confident could be overcome could easily lead to giant, relationship-destroying cracks.

Seems to me, when you love someone, you got to hold on to them. Maybe if someone had told your father that, we'd still be together now.

She closed her eyes against the sting of tears as her mom's statement replayed through her mind.

Maybe it was she, and not Jed, who resembled her father. Maybe this was something they could push through. Maybe, given time, conversation and prayer, his mother would change.

Was she shooting for perfection and, in the process, robbing herself of a second chance at love? Or was she being wise and protecting the both of them, as well as Ava, from greater heartache later?

Ducks had gathered close by. Paige stopped at a nearby bench to let Ava out of her stroller. "You want to see the duckies?"

Ava laughed and stomped her feet.

"Go ahead." Whenever the birds gathered too close, Ava grew nervous, so Paige shooed them away. But then Ava would try to approach them once again. Eventually, she grew bored or tired and started gathering acorns. Paige would allow this so long as she didn't try to eat them.

Mom used to bring Paige and her sister here often for picnics to watch for turtles and frogs in and around the lake. Then, years later, Paige brought Jed here so they could experience it together.

One time he'd brought his fishing pole with him. He'd showed her how to hold the pole and then had wrapped his arms around her as she tried to reel in an incredibly stubborn shoe in the water. They'd laughed pretty hard about that one. In the end, they'd caught little more than minnows, and Paige had gotten a slight sunburn.

What an amazing day that had been. That was when she'd known for certain she was in love, that she wanted to spend the rest of her life with Jed Gilbertson. But then Dad had left, Mom had withdrawn and everything had started to change.

Her phone rang, and she glanced at the screen. Held her breath.

Ardell.

She gave her nerves a moment to settle, lest her voice come out squeaky, and then answered. "Hello, this is Paige." As if she didn't know who was calling, but best to sound ultraprofessional.

"This is Ardell Dannheim. How are you?"

"Well, thank you." How much small talk would she have to endure before they reached the reason for her call? There were only two possibilities—she was letting Paige know if she'd gotten the job or not. "How are you?"

"Running against the clock, as always." Classical music played in the background. "I'd like to continue the conversation we had during the conference. As I mentioned, I've taken a new position with a new magazine, and I'm in the process of building a quality writing team to help us launch a sister publication."

"Windy City Whimsy?" A magazine catering to those who enjoyed following sophisticated and trendy fashions.

"Sounds like you've done your homework. Of course, this will take a great deal of time and planning to get off the ground." Clicking sounded on the other end, like that of fingers on a keyboard. "I need writers with initiative, who require minimal oversight, and whom I can trust to get the job done. I know your perseverance and work ethic." She paused. "Do you want to join my team?"

This was what she'd hoped for, but it still hit her as a shock.

The position was open but not solid. What if that sister publication failed? Would she be out of a job once again?

Lord, what should I do?

The moment she started to pray, a deep peace, mixed with longing, filled her. Like how she used to feel, sitting in church, before anger and fear had pulled her away. And yet God had remained, and had been calling her back to Him.

Was that what this was all about—her job loss, moving back to Sage Creek, reconnecting with Mrs. Tappen? And to help her mom and give sweet Ava more time with her grandmother. Seemed a lot of good was coming from what she originally saw as only hard.

Her thoughts jerked to Jed, squelching her reply. He loved her. Deeply.

And she loved him.

Enough to stay?

Yes. But did they both love each other enough to hold tightly through the hard, the painful and the unexpected?

"As you know, I love the fashion world. And this sounds like an exciting opportunity. When were you thinking you'd like me to start?"

"I imagine you'll need time to relocate and clear your responsibilities. But we have an important feature I'd love to assign to you. Could you start in two weeks?"

In case she needed to give her current employer notice. As if she'd found another job. With her script written, she didn't have much else holding her here.

Except Mom.

And Mrs. Tappen.

And the man who had captured her heart.

If she left Sage Creek, her and Jed's relationship would be over for sure. "Would I have the same salary I left with?"

Another pause. "I will send you a package with all of the particulars, via email. Read it over. Then we can set up a follow-up time to discuss it in detail."

"That sounds perfect." She ended the call feeling more

unsettled than ever. If this was the right opportunity for her, shouldn't she feel peace?

When Paige returned home, she found Mom and Mrs. Tappen talking in the yard and Jed heading to his truck. When his gaze met hers, he halted, and something in his eyes—confusion? Sorrow? Defeat?—gave her pause. For a moment, she thought he was going to approach her, and she held her breath. But then, with slumped shoulders, he got into his truck and drove away.

She knew Jed well enough to know something had happened. With the theater? She hoped not, not with all of the money he'd put into that place, and with the re-opening less than a week away. Should she call him, see if he wanted to talk things out or leave him be?

She watched until his truck drove away, and then she joined Mom and Mrs. Tappen.

She caught the tail end of their conversation. "I've always known something wasn't right." Mrs. Tappen tugged on the end of her braid. "Haven't I been saying that for a while now?"

Mom nodded. "Still, it's hard to believe your son-in-law would be caught up in something like that. I mean, I heard rumors they were having money problems, but two million dollars?" Mom shook her head. "What in the world did he do with it all?"

"From the sounds of it, he'd landed himself in a good deal of debt. Bad investments ate through his assets, but instead of acknowledging that and adjusting their life-style accordingly, he lived off credit cards."

"Now I understand why he and your daughter didn't help with the theater—financially, I mean."

"Because they didn't have the funds. Only, he couldn't admit that."

Paige looked between them. "What are you two talking about?"

They glanced her way, as if surprised to see her standing there.

Mrs. Tappen stared at her for a long time and then threw her hands up. "Might as well tell you, as you'll find out soon enough, considering it's been splattered across the news."

She went on to tell Paige about the fraud charges that had been filed against Jed's father. "If he was hurting for money that bad, he should've sold his land and all his horses."

"But," Mom said, "that'd mean admitting he'd cost his family a fortune."

Poor Jed. She needed to go to him. To talk to him. To be there for him, like she wished he'd been there for her. Like maybe he would've been, had she let him.

Chapter Twenty

After he'd dropped Grandma off at her house, Jed had headed straight to his parents' house to console his mom and find out the truth behind the headlines. Sitting at the breakfast counter, he watched his mother pace the kitchen. "What'd Dad's lawyer say?"

She shook her head and made a sobbing sound. "They've made a mistake. Your father would never do what they're accusing him of." She sat at the far end of the breakfast bar and covered her face with her hands.

"Have you talked to Christian yet?" Had his brother even heard the news?

"He's heading back from Houston now and should be here within the hour."

"Good." Regardless of how all of this played out, their mom would need all of the support she could get.

His phone chimed, and he glanced at the screen. Paige. Just the thought of her brought comfort.

He pulled up her text message. Are you okay?

He typed a response. Mom's freaking out.

Paige replied. Meet me at the Literary Sweet Spot. Hot chocolate and cinnamon roll. My treat.

He set his phone on the counter and eyed his mom.

She'd resumed pacing, mumbling something about money-hungry liars who were out to ruin her husband.

Sitting here wasn't doing his mom any good. And he needed a moment to think, to talk things out with someone who wasn't emotionally involved.

To be with the woman who could always brighten his worst day.

He glanced at the clock on the microwave. "I need to leave for a spell."

His mom whirled to face him. "What? Where?"

"I'll be back—I promise."

"Did you hear something? Who texted you just now?"

Telling her would likely only aggravate her further. He grabbed his Stetson from the hat stand, put it on and walked toward the entryway.

His mom scurried after him. "Are you going to meet with someone?" She grabbed him by the wrist. "Jed, talk to me!"

He faced her, with his jaw tight. "Let's not go borrowing trouble right now, Mom." He softened his tone. "As far as we know, Dad will be released by Sunday."

She took in a deep breath and nodded. "Of course. You're right. This is all just a big, unfortunate misunderstanding."

He stepped out the front door and nearly ran into Barb, his father's secretary, who was dressed in work attire. Why was she here? "Howdy."

Her eyes were bloodshot and rimmed with red, and dark circles hung beneath them. Tearing up, she looked from Jed to his mom. "Do you have a minute?"

His mom's posture stiffened. "Now?"

"I'm… I need to tell you something. Something I'd rather you hear from me." Her gaze zipped between them

again, and her thin brow was pinched. "Can we go inside? Please?"

Hugging her torso, Mom looked about ready to cave
in on herself. "What's going on?"

"I'm the one who called the authorities."

Jed recoiled, feeling as if he might be sick. "What are
you saying?"

"I wrestled with my decision for a long time. You
have to know I didn't want to turn your father in. But
I had to do what I felt was right. The truth was eating
away at me. And I knew, if the Feds figured out what he
was doing, and that I knew, and I didn't say anything, I
could be implicated. I can't go to jail over this. I've got
kids at home."

Jed's stomach clenched. "So you're saying the news
reports are true? And that you were involved?"

"I had nothing to do with it. I wouldn't have even
known what he was doing if I hadn't audited our finances.
My company credit card was frozen, which surprised me,
as I hardly ever use it, and never for anything significant
or out of the ordinary. So I did some digging."

"You've made a mistake." His mom's voice sounded
scratchy. "I'm sure there's a reasonable explanation."

"I wish that were the case. I really do."

Mom shook her head, her face pale. "You're lying. I
don't know what your game is, but you better leave this
house. Now."

Barb's eyes blinked rapidly, as if she were fighting to
hold herself together. "I know this is hard, but I wanted
you to hear it from me first. Before…" She took a breath.
"Before the trial."

"I said go. Otherwise my son will make you leave."

"Mom." Jed placed what he hoped to be a calming

hand on her shoulder. "What if she's telling the truth?" The genuine anguish in her eyes said she was.

He couldn't believe this was happening to his family. It was all so unreal.

Paige sat in a pale green velvet chair with her hands wrapped around a steaming vanilla latte. Across the table from her in a wingback chair with plaid upholstery, Jed stared into his mug of hot cocoa. He'd not taken a sip yet. Hadn't even touched his favorite part—the whipped cream on top.

He sighed and lifted his eyes to hers. "He could face some serious jail time."

"I'm sorry."

"And they could lose everything, including the house. Which he might deserve, but not my mom."

"Where would she go?"

"I suspect my grandma's." He scrubbed a hand over his face. "I want to believe he didn't do this, but my gut says otherwise. Still, it's hard to wrap my head around. This is something you see unfolding on television, not within your own family."

That statement couldn't be more true. Mr. Gilbertson was the picture of success. A well-respected community member and family man.

Jed rubbed his knuckles along the scruff on his jaw. "I guess I'm glad this is all coming out now, before…"

"Before what?"

"You know, that conversation we've been having."

"Before I committed my life to you, you mean?"

"You don't need this kind of mess in your life."

"Your father's poor decisions won't scare me away." Funny how she could say that without hesitation after how she'd felt regarding Jed's mom. But somehow, seeing his need, his hurt, changed everything. Urged her to hold tightly.

To be there for him.

Wasn't that what love was about? Standing by one another's side through the good and the bad?

She'd allowed her past to distort her present, and it'd nearly robbed her of her best friend. And the man she loved. She knew that now as clearly as she knew why she'd worked so hard to push him away—because love was scary. And sometimes it hurt. But maybe, just maybe, it could help them both heal, too.

"It's time I quit running scared," she said.

"What does that mean?"

She offered a shy smile.

His grin blossomed in full, but then he sobered, and his gaze intensified. "Man, you're beautiful. And kind, and smart and super talented."

Her heart squeezed, followed by a rush of panic that made her want to bolt out of her seat and hurry back to Chicago. If not for the words she'd spoken to Jed moments ago and to herself the entire drive over. She needed to let the past go, silence her fears and quit fighting what she'd known to be true all along.

This man was capturing every last piece of her heart.

The next day, Jed drove to the county jail to visit his father. He wasn't sure he wanted to go. What he wanted to do was pretend this whole mess hadn't happened, that his mom wasn't home alternating between sobbing and pacing her kitchen. That his dad would likely spend the next few years, if not more, in prison.

His law firm would go under—if he were convicted, no client in their right mind would want anything to do with him. That meant Jed's parents could lose their place, Mom would—

"You okay?" Paige, who was sitting in the passenger's seat, touched his arm.

He released a breath. Then he nodded. "Just letting my thoughts get away from me."

"I can imagine."

He looked at her. With soft ringlets framing her peach-toned face, and her delicate brows pinched above her blue eyes, she was so incredibly beautiful. Inside and out. "Thanks for being here, for coming with me."

"Of course." She twined her hand with his and gave a gentle squeeze. "I'm not going anywhere."

His heart lifted. They could talk about her plans, about their relationship, later. Right now he needed to see his dad. To get answers.

"Want me to go in with you?"

He shook his head. "This is something I need to do alone." He and his dad needed to have a serious talk.

"Can we pray?"

He studied her. Did that mean…?

She gave a soft laugh. "You act like I asked you to join me on an international mission trip or something."

"It's just…" He paused.

"That God and I weren't on speaking terms with one another?"

His mouth twitched toward a smile. "Something like that."

She shrugged. "We worked things out. Or more accurately, I decided to quit being an angry little brat."

He laughed and pulled her close. "I'd love to pray with you."

With their hands twined together, and her forehead pressed against his, he closed his eyes.

"Dear God, please be with Jed right now. Give him strength and surround him in Your love. Amen."

"Amen." His voice sounded husky. He cleared his throat. "Thanks for that."

She nodded.

He stepped out of his truck, crossed the lot and climbed the stairs of the county jail. Inside, he signed in with the receptionist, and then waited half an hour before being taken back to see his dad. Then he was led down a long hall and into a white room filled with rectangular tables. Officers stood along the bare walls, watching everyone and everything.

Jed scanned the area and made eye contact with his dad. He sat at a long rectangular table, dressed in an orange jumpsuit.

Jed approached on stiff, heavy legs and then lowered himself into a chair across from him. Warring emotions raged within: anger that his father could do this, and disbelief that he was here at all. Shock and grief. A sorrow he didn't quite understand, except to say he'd lost his dad—the man he'd always thought him to be.

"How's your mom doing?" Dad's eyes searched Jed's, as if studying his reaction.

"How do you think she is?" She'd lost her husband. And, quite likely, her way of life, everything she'd envisioned for their future.

His father winced and dropped his gaze; his shoulders stooped. When he lifted his eyes, tears were pooling behind his lashes. "I'm sorry. I didn't mean to hurt her. Didn't mean to hurt any of you."

"You did it, then? What they're accusing you of?"

Dad glanced around the room and then looked at Jed again. He pulled on his earlobe. "It's all just a big mis-

take. I mixed some numbers up, made some accounting errors."

"Two million dollars' worth?"

"Everything happened so quickly. Bills and retainers
coming in, checks going out."

"Don't lie to me." That was one thing Jed couldn't
stand, a liar. "Barb stopped by the house."

Dad blanched.

"How could you?"

"I'm sorry." He sobbed and dropped his face in his
hands. "I messed up. Big-time."

"How long? How long has this been going on?"

Dad shrugged.

"Growing up, I tried so hard to please you. To live up
to the ridiculously high standard you set. Always felt I
didn't measure up…"

"I've always been proud of you. I'm the one who's
not good enough for you. Your brother. Your mom." He
stared at his hands for a long moment, as his shoulders
were quaking. Then he swiped the back of his hand beneath his nose and raised red-rimmed eyes. "Take care
of your mom for me."

"What does that mean?"

"I don't deserve her."

Jed shoved back from the table, scraping his chair
legs against the linoleum floor, and stood. "I've heard
enough."

He half expected, maybe hoped, his dad would call
out after him. Nothing.

By the time he returned to his truck, he felt as if
every ounce of energy had been sucked out of him. The
little he'd eaten for breakfast churned in his gut. He
still couldn't believe this was happening. And yet it all
made sense.

He slid behind the steering wheel and leaned his head back against the headrest.

Paige placed a hand on his knee. "You okay?"

"I will be." He started to shift into Reverse, but then stopped, letting his arm drop. "Money's always been his top priority. I can see that now. And to think, all those years I blamed myself for the distance between us."

"It wasn't you."

"Guess I'm the one with daddy issues, huh?" Seemed he and Paige had more in common than he'd thought.

"We've all got issues." She offered a gentle smile and linked her fingers with his. "How about we work through our issues together."

"Promise?"

She hesitated just long enough to make him nervous. Releasing a breath, she nodded. "I'd like that."

He leaned toward her and cupped her chin in his hand. "I love you," he whispered.

A flash of fear filled her eyes, but she didn't pull away. He closed the distance between them and kissed her gently.

All the while praying, trusting, this wouldn't be their last. That she'd stay with him for good.

Chapter Twenty-One

A cool breeze swept over Paige, carrying with it the scent of lilacs. The thick branches of the oak tree and the clouds interspersed above them provided a wonderful reprieve from the sun's intense rays. With the cooler temperatures, she didn't feel rushed to get Ava back inside, which meant she could spend more time with Jed.

With all he and his family had experienced this week, she sensed he needed every moment of support she could offer.

Jed's chest rose and fell with his breath. "This is nice. Relaxing. I could stay here forever."

"Seems like old times, doesn't it? You and I sitting here, leaning against this gnarled tree trunk." She kissed the top of Ava's head and then nestled deeper into Jed's arms. "Although, back then our conversations centered on our dreams for the future. Boy, were we naive, huh?"

"I'd prefer to think of us as more hopeful. Things sure seemed so much simpler back then, didn't they? As if the future was ours for the taking. All we needed to do was reach for it."

She nodded. "We had it all planned out. Graduated by eighteen, married by nineteen, living in a cute little two-bedroom apartment with lace curtains and wood floors. Me pursuing a successful journalism career, while you…" She twisted to peer up at him. "You know, I can't remember you ever talking about what you wanted to do when you grew up."

He chuckled. "I was too busy obsessing over what I didn't want to do, which primarily centered on my refusal to follow in my old man's footsteps. Turns out that was a good thing. But I got to admit, never in my wildest dreams would I have considered my dad would one day be facing five to twenty years in prison, or that my mom could one day lose her home."

"And I never thought I'd be divorced, back in Sage Creek and unemployed—"

"Hey, now." He gave her a playful squeeze. "From what I've heard, you've got an amazing boss."

She grinned. "I do, though the position is temporary."

He shifted to a more upright position, jostling Ava, who'd started to doze off. "Doesn't have to be. You know that."

She studied him; his dark eyes were so earnest, pleading.

So filled with love and hope.

For her.

"Turn down the offer from Ardell." He cupped her face in his hand. "Say you'll stay. With me. I can't promise you fancy shopping malls and high-rise office buildings and paychecks to match, but I can promise to love you forever. To give my every breath to making you happy. I can promise you'll always have a safe place to land, to explore, to dream and grow."

His gaze dropped to Ava, who'd drifted back into a gentle sleep. "And I promise the same to this precious little one. Your home's here, Paige. It may not seem like much, but you have to know I'll give you all I got. I'll give that to both of you."

Her heart squeezed, and tears pricked her eyes. "It's more than enough. I can see that now."

This might not be the life she'd always dreamed of, but it was the one she wanted. The one her heart needed.

Chapter Twenty-Two

Paige chased a giggling Ava around her mother's living room. Each time she caught her, she snatched her up, swung her in the air and then placed her back onto her feet. They continued this game, with Mom watching and laughing from her recliner, until Paige's back and arms indicated she'd had enough.

"All right, munchkin. Time for your bath." Hopefully the active play, followed by warm, soothing water, would make bedtime easier. Ava hadn't been sleeping well lately, in part due to a recurring stubborn streak that seemed to emerge shortly after dinner. Apparently whatever she'd missed of the terrible twos was trying to catch up with her now, at almost three.

The doorbell rang. "I'll get it." Paige positioned Ava on her hip and crossed the room. She answered the door to find Mrs. Gilbertson standing on the stoop, wearing a floral blouse and lavender capris. With deep frown lines framing her mouth, and red lines etching the whites of her eyes, she looked about ten years older and ten times as frail.

"Is something wrong? Is Jed—"

Mrs. Gilbertson raised a hand. "No, nothing like that."

She glanced past her, at Paige's mom. "Mrs. Cordell. Paige, can we talk? Is now a good time?"

"Um… Sure." She stepped back to allow her in, but Mrs. Gilbertson remained fixed where she was.

"Actually, I was wondering…" She fiddled with her bracelet. "Perhaps we could go for a walk."

"Okay." Was she planning to tell Paige to stay away from her son? Except, the normal edge in her voice and hard glint in her eyes were gone, replaced by something much more…vulnerable.

Paige turned to her mom. "Would you mind—?"

Mom sprang to her feet. "Spend some snuggle time with my precious granddaughter?" She grinned and approached with arms opened wide. "I'd love to."

Paige gave Ava a hug, handed her off and then followed Jed's mom outside. She quietly closed the door behind them.

They walked in silence at first, and though Paige's jumbled nerves—and the countless questions running through her mind—challenged her patience, she chose not to push.

The woman had been through a lot, and regardless of how she'd treated Paige in the past, she wanted to be sensitive to that. During times like this, one needed to proceed carefully and with a heavy dose of compassion.

At the end of the sidewalk, Mrs. Gilbertson stopped. "I'm sure the irony of our situation doesn't escape you." She motioned toward an empty bench, which was flanked by flowers, and they both sat.

"Ma'am?"

"After all the ruckus I've made over the years regarding your family, turns out mine is an even bigger mess than yours. And yet, despite the news and all the gossip circulating about my husband's—" she closed her eyes, as if fighting tears "—behavior, you've demonstrated integrity and…love. A faithful, committed love my son's needed."

"I do love him. Very much."

"I know. And I'm glad."

Paige blinked. "You are?"

She nodded. "Like I said, he's needed you, and you've been there for him. You've demonstrated that you'll continue to be there, even when life becomes hard and it feels as if the world is trying to pull you both in opposite directions. That's all I've ever wanted for him." She gave a harsh laugh. "I was so convinced your family was so dysfunctional, and that ours was so much better. I've come to realize we're all a mess in our own way." She gave a wry laugh. "Making a relationship work isn't about avoiding conflict or difficulties, but learning to work through them."

"I've come to realize the same thing." Funny how similar she and Mrs. Gilbertson were. She'd been protecting her son out of fear, and Paige had been protecting herself for the same reason.

Mrs. Gilbertson straightened, and the intensity of her gaze increased. "Something I have no doubt you and Jed will do."

"What are you saying?" Was this seriously happening? Had Mrs. Gilbertson truly had a change of heart? Was she actually giving Paige her blessing to pursue a life with her son?

"What I'm saying, dear, is that I am grateful my son has you. And I'm very sorry for misjudging you."

Paige wrapped her arms around Mrs. Gilbertson before she could stop herself.

Jed's mom stiffened beneath Paige's embrace for half a breath, but then relaxed, gave Paige's shoulder a quick pat and pulled away. She composed herself, replacing the insecure and remorseful woman she'd momentarily been with the familiar matriarch. "Any other questions or concerns you feel we should discuss?"

Paige smiled. "None that I can think of."

Mrs. Gilbertson gave a curt nod and stood. She motioned toward Paige's house. "Shall we?"

On Friday evening, Jed tapped his blazer pocket, assuring himself that the tiny box remained where he'd placed it. He cast Paige a furtive glance, while feeling his stomach somersaulting worse than before his first bull ride. Even worse than the first time he'd asked Paige out on a date.

Man, were the hours dragging on. And to think, he still had to make it through an entire production at the theater.

He had it all planned. They would put on an amazing show. Everyone would congratulate her—all of them— on their hard work. Then they'd leave them alone, just him and Paige, in the business they'd resurrected, to celebrate their equally resurrected love and solidify it forever. Till death do they part.

Hopefully Paige wouldn't be tired and want to go home once the show ended. He had no doubt he could convince her to stay, but he wanted her to enjoy every moment.

He wanted the evening to be perfect. To sweep her off her feet and make her feel like the most beautiful and cherished woman in all of Texas.

Because she was.

Maybe he should wait until tomorrow. Or Sunday. Take her on a picnic or something.

Except, this felt right—to propose at the place responsible for bringing them back together. The place she'd helped save.

He checked the time on his phone. His mom wouldn't be here for at least another twenty minutes, but she was coming. She'd said so herself. And she was stopping by Grandma's to pick her up on the way.

He was still processing how much things had changed since his dad's arrest. It sure explained a lot—why his parents never helped with the theater, why his dad was always so tight-lipped about things. As though he were hiding something.

Because he had been.

To think, Paige and his mom were actually getting along. They weren't exactly chummy—at least not yet. But they seemed to hold genuine respect for one another. And he was proud of his mom. It'd taken a lot of courage for her to approach Paige, to apologize and take steps toward friendship.

Paige came over to him. "I still can't believe how wonderful everything looks." She spun in a circle, and her blue eyes were shining. "Tonight's going to be amazing."

"Thanks to you." He closed the distance between them, pulled her close to him and wrapped his arms around her slender body. He couldn't wait to see the look on her face, to see her shy yet beautiful smile emerge, when he asked for her hand. "This is it, huh?"

"Everything's going to turn out great." She smiled at him.

Man, did he love this girl. What would it be like to spend every day with her for the rest of his life? To one day hear the pitter-patter of additional pudgy feet running through the house—their house.

Just then he heard someone approach, and he turned to shake hands with Drake, the man who'd helped bring life to his vision, one two-by-four at a time. "Thanks for coming, man."

"Had to see my best work in action—when the lights are dimmed and the tables are filled." He shot Paige a wink. "Thanks for the tickets."

"My pleasure." Jed glanced around. "Want something to drink?" He motioned one of his waiters over. "Hey, Rodney, show my friend here to his seat and get him a Billy the Kid." Their house special, it was iced sweet tea with blackberry syrup and fresh, plump berries. Jed felt certain it'd be a hit.

"Will do, boss."

Hopefully their guests would enjoy the other menu changes, as well.

If he'd learned anything over the past couple of years, it was that two things could kill their business—poor food and cheesy productions.

He, Grandma and Paige had worked long and hard to rectify both. Tonight would show them how successful their efforts were.

When the two sauntered off, Paige turned to Jed. "Your mom just sent me a text. Said she's running a bit late but that they're on their way."

He grinned. "Now, there's a change."

"What's that?"

"You and my mom texting."

She shrugged. "She probably figured you'd be running around like a chicken with your head cut off, with your phone battery dead, forgotten on your desk or left somewhere random."

"You both know me well."

"Agreed." With her hands planted on her hips, she glanced around. "So…how can I help?"

"Pray? With all the publicity you managed to wrangle up, this night is too important to mess up."

"Relax. Everything's going to be amazing. I have no doubt." She gave him a quick kiss on the cheek.

He'd spend the rest of his life doing all he could to ensure she always looked at him with the same love and admiration her eyes held now.

Paige sat at a table near the front of the theater with her eyes trained on the entrance. She stood when Jed's grandmother and mother entered, anxious to greet them. In part because she knew his mom would be nervous, wondering what everyone might be saying about her and her husband. As if the pain of it all weren't enough, some were accusing her of being complicit, saying she had to have known about her husband's illegal activities.

But others, like Mrs. Tappen's quilting friends, surrounded and supported her.

In fact, that was how most of Sage Creek responded. True, there were those who enjoyed a juicy piece of gossip, finding entertainment in another's pain. But most banded together to love on one of their own.

She hadn't realized until now how much she'd missed that. Chicago's fine restaurants, museums and shopping malls were great, but they couldn't replace the bonds that united folks here.

That was the type of security, the sense of belonging, she hoped Ava would grow up experiencing.

She smoothed wrinkles from the front of her blouse, wove around occupied tables and strolled forward. "Mrs. Tappen. Mrs. Gilbertson."

Jed's grandmother pulled her into a tight hug. "So good to see you, dear." With her eyes dancing, she held Paige by the arms and then released her.

Paige shifted to face Mrs. Gilbertson with her hand extended. "Ma'am. I'm so glad you could come."

"Good to see you, Paige." She looked around. Her gaze lingered on the stage with its general-store background, hitching rail bordering the right and covered wagon decorating the left. "This place truly looks spectacular."

Mrs. Tappen beamed. "Agreed. That boy of yours has quite an imagination. And wait until you see the show. Paige here wrote up quite a doozy. Folks're gonna have to use their noggin' overtime to solve the mystery she's come up with."

"I have no doubt." The admiration in her eyes warmed Paige.

"Matter of fact, let's get a program," Mrs. Tappen said. "After the show, maybe our star writer will sign them for us." She winked, and Paige blushed.

It felt nice to be praised by Jed's grandmother, especially in front of his mom.

While the two women traipsed off, Paige returned to her seat, anxious for the show to begin.

Jed rushed from place to place—into the kitchen, backstage, out to the lobby, back to his office—casting frequent nervous glances her way. He was adorable. She loved the take-charge energy he showed when tackling a problem, caring for his grandmother or mowing Mom's yard, and now dealing with staff and last-minute production details.

Mrs. Tappen and Mrs. Gilbertson returned. His grandmother sat to Paige's right, while his mom sat one chair beyond that. The women talked about past shows, the costumes, what happened behind the scenes. As the last of the patrons arrived, excited chatter, giggles and the clanking of glasses on wooden tabletops swirled through the paneled room.

Then the show began. Jed started things off, cracking some jokes and thanking everyone for being there. He looked more handsome than ever in his Stetson, leather vest, chaps and boots. He'd just begun to launch into the backstory of the local saloon owner, a woman with a questionable past, when two gunslingers tromped onstage.

"Keep your eye on the man with the mustache." The taller of the two leaned toward his friend, motioning with his head toward a tall, bald-headed guy in the audience.

The other gunslinger nodded. "Feller looks shifty, all right. Pro'ly on Sheriff Brewster's payroll."

Laughter filled the room as the story unfolded, with all of its clues, puns and mishaps, Paige's heart swelled. Everything was turning out better than she'd expected.

Was Jed pleased? She looked about, hoping to catch a glimpse of him.

When the sheriff challenged the suspected murderer to a draw, and the saloon owner ran through the audience in search of a pencil and paper, Mrs. Tappen bent over with laughter. "Girl—" she patted Paige's knee "—you found your thing."

Paige smiled. "Thanks. I sure seem to have stumbled into something. Me, a scriptwriter—who knew?" Something she could see herself doing well into her golden years. This was much better than working for Ardell. As hard and frightening as it'd been to turn down the job offer, Paige knew she'd done the right thing.

"God knew all along." Mrs. Tappen gave her leg another pat. "You didn't stumble into nothing, sweet pea."

She angled her head. "I don't understand."

"Jeremiah 29:11."

Paige's confusion must have shown on her face, because Mrs. Tappen said, "'For I know the plans I have for you,' says the Lord. 'They are plans for good.' Mmm-hmm. 'To give you hope and a future.'"

A future. With Jed? *Lord, is that why You brought me back here? To heal me and to heal us?*

All of this time, she'd been trying to plan her own way, her own life—running from the man she most loved. Meanwhile God had been working things out on her behalf, to give her back what she'd nearly lost forever.

Thank You, Lord. From now on, I'll leave the planning to You.

While half the cast fought, wrestled and hollered with one another upstage left, Jed sauntered out. "Now comes the time you've all been waiting, working and thinking-on for." His eyes danced when they landed on Paige, and for a moment he faltered. Reminding her of how tentative he was on the night of their first date.

"Hopefully you've been keeping track of clues, watching suspects… By a show of hands—don't shout it out, now—how many of you think you know who the killer is?"

People glanced about. Some shot their hands up.

"All righty, then. Go ahead and write down who. Also, why you think he or she or they did it—that's cowboy talk for *motive*. And why this is the best show you've seen this side of the Rio Grande."

Someone from the back whooped at that one, and applause sounded.

"But first I want to thank a special lady for helping to make all this happen. Without her hard work, all we'd have is a purty building and some great steaks."

Oh, no. Paige sank in her seat, trying to be as inconspicuous as possible. Surely he didn't mean—

"Scriptwriter Paige Cordell is as talented as they come. Funny, clever, knows how to spin a tale, and I'm betting with all her red herrings—that's writer talk for false clues…" He shot her a wink. "She made most of you guess wrong in regard to who the killer is. Help me thank her good and proper."

The applause increased as everyone jumped to their feet.

Tears stung Paige's eyes as they met Jed's. "Thanks," she mouthed.

She knew now, with more certainty than she'd ever felt previously, she belonged here, in Sage Creek, with her friends, her church family, her mom and Mrs. Tappen…

And Jed.

Chapter Twenty-Three

Jed walked the *Sage Creek Herald*'s reporter to the door and shook his hand. "Thank you for coming."

Keith Gray secured the lens cap on his camera. "It was a great show. Look for the story in tomorrow's paper. Who knows, might even make the front cover."

"That'd be awesome." He held the door open for him, tipped his hat and then slipped back inside to where Paige waited.

His beautiful princess was watching him with those adoring eyes that always melted his insides.

He crossed the lobby to meet her and took her hands in his. "What do you say we celebrate a night well-done?"

She angled her head. "What do you have in mind?"

"Come on." He guided her back into the theater, now dim, and to a central table that had been cleared and cleaned. He pulled out a chair for her. "I'll be right back."

He dashed into the kitchen and to the dessert he'd asked his chef to prepare—a signature dish that merged all her favorite flavors—a mousse tower with chocolate wafers, mint garnish, drizzled in salted caramel.

And hidden within the decadent cream—his grandmother's engagement ring.

He tucked a small book of matches in his pocket, grabbed a long-stemmed candle in a silver holder with one hand, the dessert and two spoons to share it in the other, and headed back to his love.

She offered the most radiant smile. "What's this?"

"Something sweet for you." He set it in front of her, placed the candle in the center of the table and lit it. "But first…" He pulled out his phone and clicked on his radio app. "May I have this dance?"

She gave a soft laugh. "I'd be honored." She stood, and placing her hand in his, allowed him to lead her to an open area between tables. As they danced, she rested her head against his chest, and her vanilla-cinnamon perfume tickled his nose.

She peered up at him with those big blue eyes. "We've come a long way."

"Oh, Paige, we're just getting started." As one song transitioned to another, he led her back to their table and their dessert.

She took a bite and closed her eyes. "This is amazing." She looked at him again. "You're something else—you know that, Jed Gilbertson?"

"I'll be whatever you want me to be. Whatever I can do to see your face light up, to see that beautiful smile of yours." He glanced at the plate, still filled with three quarters of a mousse. Why had he placed the ring in the dessert? It was taking too long to get to it.

Time to speed things along.

He sliced through the whipped cream with his spoon, pulled out the ring, wiped it clean as best as he could with a napkin and then dropped to one knee beside her. "The execution might leave a little to be desired." He gave a sheepish smile. "But…"

She gasped. "Is that…?"

"Grandma's ring?" He nodded. "She's been holding on to it. For you." Seemed she knew Paige was the one for him long before either of them did. "I'm not sure exactly when I fell in love with you. One day you were the curly-haired girl who lived next to my grandma and loved to make mud pies and catch frogs. The next you were the girl who occupied my dreams."

He tucked a curl behind her ear and then brushed her cheek with his knuckles. "My heart broke the day you left, and I thought I'd lost you. But then you came back. To me. And my world felt right again."

"Oh, Jed." A tear slid down her cheek, and he thumbed it away.

"I can't live without you, Paige. I love you more than life itself, and I plan to spend the rest of my days proving just how much, if you'll let me. Will you marry me, Paige?"

He held his breath as her eyes searched his. But then she squealed, "Yes. A thousand times yes."

Epilogue

Butterflies fluttered in Paige's stomach as she waited in the choir room for her wedding music to start. How many times in high school had she imagined this day—the moment when Jed pledged to love her for the rest of her life? After all that had happened, between her and Jed, with her divorce, she struggled to believe this day had actually arrived. In less than an hour, she'd leave Trinity Faith Church as Mrs. Jed Gilbertson.

The door creaked open, and Mom entered with Ava in her arms. "Look who's awake." Wearing a white dress with lace trim and a wide pink bow, and with soft curls framing her face, she resembled a cupid.

"Isn't she the sweetest?" Mrs. Tappen held out her arms, and Mom handed Ava over.

"Much thanks to our resident seamstress." Mom smiled at her longtime friend.

Paige's wedding dress, worn first by Mrs. Tappen, then adapted and worn by Jed's mom, was perfect. They'd removed the sleeves, altered the waist and added some delicate beading, while retaining its simple elegance. What made Paige feel most cherished, however, was the generations of love and strength the gown had come to represent.

Mom took Paige's hands in hers. "You look absolutely radiant."

"Agreed." Mrs. Tappen stepped forward, wrapped an arm around Paige's waist and squeezed. "That grandson of mine is a lucky man."

The organ music started, and her sister Anneliese rushed in with wide eyes and flushed cheeks. "You ready?" She glanced about, picked up Ava's flower basket and held it out to her. But Ava seemed more interested in fiddling with her shoelaces.

"Guess this is it." Paige fanned her face.

"Smile!" Mira snapped four photos in rapid succession and then grabbed her bouquet. "See you on the other side." Then she and the rest of the party began their march, soon leaving Paige and her uncle standing side by side.

"You ready, kiddo?"

"Beyond ready," she said. "Thanks for coming."

"Wouldn't miss this for the world. We're up." He led her out the door, through the foyer and into the sanctuary filled with friends Paige had known since as long as she could remember. White tulle and the most beautiful peach carnations decorated the pews, and silk petals dotted the carpet before her.

Halfway down the aisle, Ava appeared to have grown bored of her flower-girl duties, had deposited an overturned basket near the second row and now sat on Mrs. Tappen's lap.

Paige laughed, then lifted her gaze to meet Jed's. Dressed in a perfectly tailored tuxedo and his signature boots and Stetson, he watched her with a love and an adoration that stole her breath.

* * *

Jed felt almost heady watching his beautiful bride gliding toward him. Soon she was standing before him, peering up at him with her blue eyes, which were full of trust, and he was determined to spend the rest of his life proving himself worthy.

Never would she want for anything. He'd make sure of that.

Pastor Roger read from 1 Corinthians, and then Paige read a poem she'd written, which spoke of how love had basically smacked her in the head and taken her captive. Half of the patrons seemed to give a collective sigh.

He winked at her and then pulled his vows from his pocket. "What I've got to say isn't quite so eloquent, but every word comes from right here." He patted his chest.

He took her hands in his. "I'm not sure when it happened. But one day I was tugging your braids and chasing after you with earthworms. The next I never could catch my breath when you were around. You filled my thoughts, my dreams. Made me want to be a better man.

"My world ended the day you left Texas," he continued. "And it turned bright again when you came back. I started dreaming of you and me, sipping coffee on the porch together, of countless nights sitting before a roaring fire, with you in my arms."

He turned to Ava, who now sat on the floor a few feet away from them. "Of me striving to be the best father to this little girl that a man can be in the hopes that one day she'll choose me as her daddy."

"Oh, Jed!" Paige thumbed tears from beneath her eyes.

"But mostly—" he took her hands in his once again "—I plan on spending every moment the good Lord allows enjoying the treasure He's given me in you. Because I for sure know I don't deserve you."

He accepted the ring from his groomsman. Then, with his gaze locked on Paige's, he slipped the wedding ring onto her finger. "With this ring, Paige Cordell, I claim you as mine, now and forever. To hold, to cherish, to protect and to provide for, all the days of my life."

Then it was Paige's turn. "With this ring, I bind myself to you, Jed Gilbertson. I'll honor, respect, encourage and support you. And I'll spend every day of the rest of my life building a future with the best man a woman could hope for."

"Well, then," the pastor said, "by the powers vested in me by the state of Texas, I now pronounce you husband and wife. Jed, my friend, you may now kiss your beautiful bride."

Jed grinned, pulled Paige close and planted a kiss on her lips, knowing this moment was but the first of many as Mr. and Mrs. Gilbertson.

* * * * *

If you enjoyed Hometown Healing,
look for Jennifer Slattery's earlier book
Restoring Her Faith

Available now from Love Inspired!

Find more great reads at
www.LoveInspired.com

Note to the Reader

Paige's mother suffers from Somatization Disorder, a mental illness in which the individual experiences physical symptoms caused by mental factors. She expresses physical symptoms that appear to have no medical origin. You may be more familiar with the term *hypochondria*, which is a psychosomatic illness. It is a debilitating and pervasive fear in which the person believes they have a serious and undiagnosed illness. I've seen how devastating this illness can be in the lives of loved ones, so I understand Paige and her mother. One might think the easiest solution would be to convince the individual that she isn't indeed sick, but as with other mental illnesses, somatization disorder is complicated and difficult to treat. But perhaps the best thing we can do for our friends and loved ones with this condition is to show compassion, as Paige is trying to do. We don't have to fully understand someone in order to love them.

Dear Reader,

I visited my first murder mystery dinner theater around twenty years ago. I was newly married, went with my husband, and laughed and laughed when he was unexpectedly pulled into the performance. Since then, we were hooked and have sought out various dinner theaters while on vacation. They combine two of my loves—story and food!

As I was considering both Jed and Paige's problems, an idea formed that merged the two aforementioned loves with a third—my affinity for all things Texas. The result: a small-town story centered on Texas-sized dreams and the love that ties them both together. I hope you enjoy *Hometown Healing* and feel inspired to pursue your own dreams.

Jennifer

THE AMISH CHRISTMAS MATCHMAKER

Indiana Amish Brides • by Vannetta Chapman

When Annie Kauffmann's father decides to join Levi Lapp in Texas to start a new Amish community, Annie doesn't want to go. Her wedding business is in Indiana, so leaving's out of the question. But if Annie finds Levi a wife, he might just give up this dream of moving...

HER AMISH HOLIDAY SUITOR

Amish Country Courtships • by Carrie Lighte

A pretend courtship with Lucy Knepp's just the cover Nick Burkholder needs to repair the cabin his brother damaged. And agreeing means Lucy can skip holiday festivities to work on embroidery for a Christmas fund-raiser. Will a fake courtship between this quiet Amish woman and the unpredictable bachelor turn real?

HIS UNEXPECTED RETURN

Red Dog Ranch • by Jessica Keller

For five years, Wade Jarrett's family and ex-girlfriend believed he was dead—until he returns to the family ranch. He knew he'd have to make amends...but he never expected he had a daughter. Can Wade convince Cassidy Danvers he's a changed man who deserves the title of daddy and, possibly, husband?

THEIR CHRISTMAS PRAYER

by Myra Johnson

Pastor Shaun O'Grady is ready for his next missionary assignment...until he begins working with Brooke Willoughby on the church's Christmas outreach program. Now Shaun is not quite sure where he belongs: overseas on his mission trip, or right here by Brooke's side.

THE HOLIDAY SECRET

Castle Falls • by Kathryn Springer

In her birth family's hometown, Ellery Marshall plans to keep her identity hidden until she learns more about them. But that's easier said than done when single dad Carter Bristow and his little girl begin to tug at her heart. Could she unite two families by Christmas?

THE TWIN BARGAIN

by Lisa Carter

After her babysitter's injured, Amber Fleming's surprised when the woman's grandson offers to help care for her twins while she attends nursing school...until he proposes a bargain. He'll watch the girls, if she'll use her nursing skills to care for his grandmother. But can they keep the arrangement strictly professional?

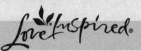
*Could a pretend Christmastime courtship
lead to a forever match?*

Read on for a sneak preview of
Her Amish Holiday Suitor, *part of Carrie Lighte's
Amish Country Courtships miniseries.*

Nick took his seat next to her and picked up the reins,
but before moving onward, he said, "I don't understand it,
Lucy. Why is my caring about you such an awful thing?"
His voice was quivering and Lucy felt a pang of guilt. She
knew she was overreacting. Rather, she was reacting to
a heartache that had plagued her for years, not one Nick
had caused that evening.

"I don't expect you to understand," she said, wiping
her rough woolen mitten across her cheeks.

"But I want to. Can't you explain it to me?"

Nick's voice was so forlorn Lucy let her defenses drop.
"I've always been treated like this, my entire life. *Lucy's
too weak, too fragile, too small, she can't go outside or
run around or have any fun because she'll get sick. She'll
stop breathing. She'll wind up in the hospital.* My whole
life, Nick. And then the one little taste of utter abandon I
ever experienced—charging through the dark with a frosty
wind whisking against my face, feeling totally invigorated
and alive… You want to take that away from me, too."

She was crying so hard her words were barely
intelligible, but Nick didn't interrupt or attempt to quiet
her. When she finally settled down and could speak

normally again, she sniffed and asked, "May I use your handkerchief, please?"

"Sorry, I don't have one," Nick said. "But here, you can use my scarf. I don't mind."

The offer to use Nick's scarf to dry her eyes and blow her nose was so ridiculous and sweet all at once it caused Lucy to chuckle. "*Neh*, that's okay," she said, removing her mittens to dab her eyes with her bare fingers.

"I really am sorry," he repeated.

Lucy was embarrassed. "That's all right. I've stopped blubbering. I don't need a handkerchief after all."

"*Neh*, I mean I'm sorry I treated you in a way that made you feel…the way you feel. I didn't mean to. I was concerned. I care about you and I wouldn't want anything to happen to you. I especially wouldn't want to play a role in hurting you."

Lucy was overwhelmed by his words. No man had ever said anything like that to her before, even in friendship. "It's not your fault," she said. "And I do appreciate that you care. But I'm not as fragile as you think I am."

"Fragile? You? I don't think you're fragile at all, even if you are prone to pneumonia." Nick scoffed. "I think you're one of the most resilient women I've ever known."

Lucy was overwhelmed again. If this kept up, she was going to fall hard for Nick Burkholder. Maybe she already had.

Don't miss
Her Amish Holiday Suitor *by Carrie Lighte,*
available October 2019 wherever
Love Inspired® books and ebooks are sold.

www.LoveInspired.com